A FAMILY'S FIGHT FOR SURVIVAL

SYBIL COOK

CHAPTER 1

CHAPTER 1

"For heaven's sake, Iris, the rooster hasn't even cleared his throat yet." Anna's voice was muffled by the pillow she'd pulled over her head, a tuft of brown curls peeking out from underneath.

Iris suppressed another cough, her chest tight as she lit the bedside lamp. The flame cast dancing shadows across their shared bedroom, illuminating the worn floorboards and faded wallpaper. "Pigs don't feed themselves, little bug. Come on, help me make breakfast."

"You never rest." Anna emerged from her cocoon

of blankets, her freckled face scrunched in protest. "You were coughing all night again."

"I'm fine." Iris waved off her sister's concern, though the tickle in her throat suggested otherwise. She pulled on her work boots, trying to ignore the heaviness in her limbs. Years of work at the farm were catching up with her.

"You're not fine." Anna's bare feet hit the cold floor with a soft thud. "You're sick."

"It's just a cold." Iris straightened up, forcing a smile. "Nothing to worry about."

Anna didn't look convinced, but she padded across the room and started pulling on her own clothes. Iris headed for the door, and the sound of smaller footsteps followed close behind.

At the back door, Iris turned to find Anna practically on her heels, already wrapped in her oversized coat. "And where do you think you're going?"

Anna lifted her chin, a determined glint in her eye that reminded Iris so much of their mother. "To feed the pigs with you. It's time I learned how to do it properly. I can't let you do everything alone anymore."

The words warmed Iris her more effectively than any medicine could. She reached out and pulled

Anna into a tight hug, pressing a kiss to the top of her head.

"Ugh, get off!" Anna squirmed away, wiping at her face dramatically. "You're so embarrassing!"

Iris couldn't help but laugh as her sister darted out the door, her too-big boots clomping across the porch. The sound of Anna's retreat echoed in the and for a moment, Iris forgot about her aching chest and tired bones. Maybe sharing the load wouldn't be such a bad thing after all.

The morning air was crisp, biting at their cheeks as Iris and Anna trudged towards the pig pen. The sun was just beginning to rise, casting a pale golden hue over the frost-covered ground. Their breath formed little clouds in the cold, each step crunching underfoot.

Anna struggled to keep up with her sister's pace, her too-big boots flopping with each step. "Iris," she started, huffing slightly from the effort, "is this really what you want?"

Iris paused mid-step, glancing back at her sister with a puzzled expression. "What do you mean?"

"This," Anna gestured around them, her small hand sweeping over the expanse of their farm. "This life. You barely have any life outside of it. You don't go to any of the harvest dance or balls or have friends because you're always here... in the pig pen."

Iris sighed, turning back to face the pen. "There's nothing I can do about it, Anna. The farm needs tending to."

Anna frowned, determination flashing in her eyes. "We could hire help."

"With what money?" Iris asked, exasperation creeping into her voice as she reached for the feed bucket. "We barely make enough to keep ourselves fed and clothed. Hiring help isn't an option."

"But I don't want to be tied here by farm work forever," Anna protested, crossing her arms stubbornly.

Iris stopped what she was doing and turned to face Anna fully, her expression softening. She placed a hand on Anna's shoulder and squeezed gently. "You won't be, Anna. Soon you'll start attending school in town like your friends."

"Really, you mean it?"

"Of course I mean it. Did you think I'd let my brilliant little sister miss out on an education?"

"But what about the farm work?"

"I'll manage." Iris tweaked her nose. "Besides, you'll still be here to help mornings and evenings. Now come on, let's get back to work."

They finished their chores in silence, though Iris couldn't help noticing Anna's lighter step and the small smile that kept creeping onto her face.

"Race you to the house?" Anna challenged as they put away their tools.

"Only if you're ready to lose," Iris said, but Anna was already running, her boots kicking up dirt behind her.

In the kitchen, they fell into their usual breakfast routine. Anna cracked eggs while Iris stoked the stove fire.

"Can I invite Sarah over after school starts?" Anna asked, fishing out a piece of shell from the bowl.

"As long as you finish your chores first." Iris mixed flour for biscuits, a small cloud rising around her hands.

"And maybe we could all go to the harvest dance next month? You, me, and Sarah's family?"

Iris hesitated, her hands stilling in the dough.

"Please?" Anna drew out the word. "You could wear Mother's blue dress. The pretty one."

"We'll see." But Iris was smiling, and Anna knew that meant yes.

Heavy footsteps creaked down the wooden stairs, and their father appeared in the kitchen doorway.

His weathered face brightened at the sight of his daughters.

"Something smells good in here." He settled into his usual chair at the head of the table, running a hand through his graying hair.

"Biscuits and eggs," Anna announced proudly, setting a plate in front of him. "I only got three pieces of shell in the bowl this time."

"That's progress." He chuckled, reaching for the butter. "Listen, girls. I'm heading to market today. Got four pigs ready to sell."

Iris placed the last batch of biscuits on the table. "The Berkshires?"

"Those are the ones. Should fetch a good price too - they're prime stock."

"I'll come with you." Iris sat down across from him. "The feed merchant still owes us from last month's delivery. I want to make sure he settles up."

Their father nodded, mouth full of biscuit. "Could use the help loading them too."

"Can I come?" Anna bounced in her seat, sending her fork clattering to the floor.

"Not today, bug." Iris shook her head. "I need you here."

Anna's face fell. "But-"

"I've got some books laid out for you upstairs."

Iris cut off the protest. "Your reading needs work before school starts."

"Reading is boring," Anna muttered, stabbing at her eggs.

Their father cleared his throat. "Your sister's right. Education comes first."

"Fine." Anna slumped in her chair. "But I'm not doing the dishes."

"Yes, you are." Iris fixed her with a stern look. "Dishes first, then books."

"You're worse than Mother ever was." But there was no real heat in Anna's words.

Their father's eyes crinkled at the corners. "Your mother would be proud of you both."

Iris ducked her head, focusing on her plate. "What time do you want to leave for market?"

"Hour's time should do it." He pushed back from the table. "I'll get the wagon ready."

"I'll help as soon as I'm done here." Iris gathered the empty plates. "Anna, don't forget - dishes, then straight upstairs to study."

Anna made a face but grabbed a dish towel. "Will you at least tell me about the market when you get back?"

"Every detail," Iris promised. "Even the boring parts about feed prices."

"That's not what I meant, and you know it." Anna flicked soap suds at her sister. "I want to hear about the people and the music and-"

"The dishes," Iris reminded her firmly. "Focus on what's in front of you first."

Heavy footsteps creaked down the wooden stairs, and their father appeared in the doorway, already dressed for the day's work. His weathered face brightened at the sight of his daughters in the kitchen.

"Something smells good in here," he said, settling into his usual chair at the head of the table.

"Iris made biscuits," Anna announced, sliding a plate in front of him. "And I did the eggs all by myself."

"Only dropped two shells this time," Iris added with a wink.

Their father chuckled. "You're getting better every day, Anna." He took a bite of his breakfast and nodded approvingly. "Speaking of getting better, I've got some news. Planning to take four of our pigs to market today."

Iris looked up from her plate. "Four? I thought we were only selling two."

"Price is good right now. Better to sell while we can get top dollar." He spread butter on his biscuit.

"Besides, winter's coming. We could use the extra money for repairs."

"I'll go with you," Iris said quickly. "The loading will be easier with two people."

Their father nodded. "Could use the help. Market's busy on Thursdays."

"Can I come too?" Anna perked up, nearly knocking over her glass of milk in her excitement.

"Not today, bug," Iris said. "I need you here. There are some books upstairs I want you to look at. Practice your reading while we're gone."

Anna's face fell. "But I want to see the market."

"The books are important," Iris insisted. "And I need you to wash up after breakfast. We'll be back before you know it."

"Promise?"

"Cross my heart." Iris drew an X over her chest. "And if you finish the chapter I marked, maybe we can talk about that harvest dance you mentioned."

Anna brightened immediately. "Really?"

"Only if those dishes are spotless and you've done your reading," their father added, catching on quickly.

"I'll do them right now!" Anna jumped up, gathering plates with newfound enthusiasm.

"Careful with those," Iris cautioned, but she was

smiling. "The books are on my bed. Start with the blue one - I've marked the pages."

Their father finished his coffee and stood. "Better get the wagon ready. Iris, you good to head out in twenty minutes?"

"I'll be ready," she said, already moving to help Anna with the dishes. "Just need to change into something more suitable for market."

The wagon creaked under the weight of fifteen pigs as Iris and Henry made their way down the dirt road. Iris gripped the reins, steering the horses around a particularly deep rut while her father checked their cargo.

"Careful there," Henry said, steadying himself against the wooden seat. "Last thing we need is a broken wheel before market."

Iris nodded, her eyes fixed on the road ahead. She watched a group of Turner wagons pass them by, their new covered transport systems protecting their pigs from the morning chill. "Father, have you seen how well the Turners' pigs sold last month?"

"Heard about it." Henry adjusted his cap against the wind. "Got themselves some fancy new setup, from what I gather."

"It's not just fancy." Iris pulled back on the reins as they approached a steep incline. "They've got this new feeding system. Myariah told me they're using different grain combinations, and they've built these special pens that keep the pigs warmer in winter."

Henry's jaw tightened. "The Turners have always had money to throw around."

"But it's working." Iris gestured to another Turner wagon passing them. "Their pigs gained weight faster, and they sold for almost double what we're getting."

"And how much do you reckon that setup cost them?" Henry patted the side of their worn wagon. "We can barely afford new wheels for this old girl."

"At this rate, we won't be able to afford feed by winter's end." Iris straightened her back. "We lost three piglets last month alone."

"We've managed before." Henry crossed his arms. "We'll manage again."

"Managing isn't enough anymore." Iris checked on their pigs through a gap in the wagon's slats. "The market's changing. Everyone else is adapting-"

"We can't afford to adapt right now, Iris." Henry said with a note of finality. "That's the end of it."

Iris pressed her lips together and focused on steering around another pothole. The rest of their journey continued in silence, broken only by the occasional grunt from their cargo and the steady clip-clop of hooves on packed dirt.

The market buzzed with activity as Iris and her father guided their wagon into an open space. They maneuvered carefully, the old wooden wheels creaking under the weight of their pigs. Iris hopped down first, grabbing the rope to secure their spot.

"Over here," she called, gesturing to her father to bring the pigs closer. The bustling market was alive with vendors hawking their wares, and buyers haggling for the best prices. It should have felt promising, but instead, Iris felt a knot of anxiety tighten in her chest.

Henry began unloading the pigs. "Let's get these beauties set up."

Iris nodded, though she couldn't shake her worry. They arranged their stall as neatly as possible, trying to showcase the pigs in a way that would catch buyers' eyes.

"Morning, Henry," a voice called out. Mr. Thompson, a fellow farmer, approached with a friendly nod.

"Morning," Henry replied. "Here to sell today?"

Thompson shook his head. "Just browsing. Prices are tough this season."

Iris watched as Thompson's gaze lingered on

their pigs before moving on without another word. She sighed inwardly.

The first potential buyer of the day approached. He was a stout man, and he inspected the pigs with an air of authority.

"How much for this one?" he asked, pointing to their largest pig.

Henry straightened up. "That's our best pig. We're asking fifteen shillings."

The man snorted. "Fifteen? I'll give you ten."

Iris bristled at the offer but held her tongue as Henry shook his head. "Can't go that low."

The man shrugged and moved on without another word.

As the morning wore on, it became clear that today would be no different from their recent struggles. Potential buyers haggled relentlessly, offering prices that barely covered costs. Even their best pig failed to fetch more than ten shillings.

"Iris," Henry said quietly during a lull in traffic, "we may have to accept what we can get today."

"I know," she replied through gritted teeth. "But it shouldn't be like this."

Just then, Iris overheard a wealthy landowner speaking loudly to his companion nearby. His voice dripped with disdain as he glanced over at their stall.

"Look at that stock," he scoffed. "Struggling farmers trying to pass off second-rate animals as prime quality."

Iris felt a hot flush of anger and embarrassment spread across her cheeks but forced herself to focus on the task at hand. They needed to sell these pigs, no matter what it took.

By late afternoon, they'd sold all their pigs at painfully low prices. Iris clenched her fists at her sides, fighting back tears of frustration and humiliation.

Henry placed a hand on her shoulder as they packed up their now-empty wagon. "We'll figure something out," he said quietly.

Iris nodded but couldn't find words to respond. She climbed into the wagon beside her father and stared out at the passing countryside in silence as they made their way home.

Iris and her father returned to the farm as dusk settled over the fields. The sky was painted in shades of pink and orange, but Iris couldn't find any beauty in it. The market had been a disaster.

Henry climbed down from the wagon. "I'll take care of the horses," he said

"I'll start dinner," Iris replied, her tone equally drained.

She walked into the kitchen, her legs feeling like lead. Anna was already there, setting the table with a determined look on her face.

"How was the market?"

"Not great," Iris admitted, moving to the stove to check on the stew she had left simmering. "We sold the pigs, but not for as much as we hoped."

Anna's face fell. "I'm sorry."

"It's not your fault," Iris said, stirring the pot. "We'll manage."

Henry entered the kitchen. "I'm going to my room," he announced. "Call me when dinner's ready."

Iris nodded, watching him go before turning back to Anna. "Can you get the bread from the pantry?"

"Sure." Anna moved quickly, eager to help.

Iris coughed suddenly, a harsh sound that made Anna look up in concern.

"You're still coughing?" Anna asked.

"I'm fine," Iris replied, though her voice sounded weak even to her own ears. She ignored the dizziness that swept over her and focused on finishing dinner.

Anna brought the bread to the table and started slicing it. "Do you think we'll have enough money for repairs?"

"We'll make do," Iris said, though she wasn't sure how true that was. She felt another wave of dizziness and gripped the edge of the counter to steady herself.

Anna frowned as she watched her sister. "You don't look so good."

"I'm just tired," Iris said dismissively.

"Iris?" Anna's voice sounded distant as if coming from far away.

Iris tried to respond but found she couldn't form words. Her vision blurred, and she felt herself swaying.

Anna jumped up from her seat. "Iris!"

Iris heard the shout just before everything went dark.

CHAPTER 2

CHAPTER 2

*J*ames wiped the sweat from his brow as he heaved another pile of hay into the horse's stall. Edward, his constant companion in these daily tasks, whistled a cheerful tune while spreading fresh straw for the pigs.

"I reckon these pigs eat better than my own wife's cooking," Edward said, grinning as he tossed an apple to a particularly eager sow.

James chuckled, patting the neck of a chestnut mare. "Your wife would box your ears if she heard that."

"She'd have to catch me first." Edward straightened up, brushing hay from his worn trousers. "Did you see what they're serving at the new tavern in town? Proper roasted beef, they say."

"Some of us save our coins instead of spending them on fancy meals," James replied, checking the water trough.

A commotion from the chicken coop drew their attention. Edward rushed over, waving his arms at a fox trying to sneak through a gap in the fence. "Oi! Get away from there, you mangy thing!"

James grabbed a bucket and joined the chase, the fox darting away into the undergrowth. "Third time this week. We'll need to patch that fence properly."

"Add it to the list," Edward said, already collecting tools. "Right after fixing the stable roof and that broken wagon wheel."

The sound of approaching footsteps made them both turn. Mr. Patterson, the farm owner, stood in the doorway, his usual jovial expression replaced by something more somber. His fingers worried the brim of his hat.

"James, Edward," he called out, voice unusually tight. "A word, if you please."

James set down his pitchfork, exchanging a quick

glance with Edward. They approached their employer, boots scuffing against the wooden floor.

"Sir?" James said, standing straight despite his aching back.

"I'll be direct with you boys." Patterson cleared his throat. "I've sold the farm. Papers were signed yesterday."

The words hit James like a physical blow. Edward's whistle cut off mid-note.

"Sold it?" Edward's voice cracked. "To whom?"

"Lord Ashworth. He's planning to turn it into a hunting estate." Patterson's eyes darted between them. "I'm sorry, lads. You'll have your two weeks' wages, of course, but after that..."

James forced himself to speak past the tightness in his throat. "When do we need to leave?"

"End of the day. New owner wants to start renovations immediately." Patterson pulled two envelopes from his coat. "Here's your pay. You've both been excellent workers. I'll write references, of course."

Edward took his envelope with trembling fingers. "End of the day? But what about the animals and the harvest?"

"Not our concern anymore, I'm afraid." Patterson's shoulders slumped. "Lord Ashworth has his own plans."

James accepted his envelope. Six years of work, gone in an instant. "Thank you for the opportunity, sir. And the warning."

Patterson nodded, turned to leave, then paused. "The new owner... he's not one for sentiment. Best gather your things quickly."

They watched him walk away, as the horses nickered softly in their stalls, unaware of the change in their futures.

"Well," Edward said finally, staring at his envelope, "I suppose my wife's cooking doesn't sound so bad now."

James leaned against a post, the rough wood grounding him. "We should start packing."

"What will you do?"

"Find another position, I suppose." James straightened up, his practical nature taking over. "There's always work for those willing to do it."

Edward clapped him on the back as they started walking back towards their equipment shed.

"There always is," Edward agreed brightly.

James nodded mutely. Fate itself was laughing cruel joke at his expense.

James and Edward trudged down the dirt road,

their meager belongings stuffed into canvas bags slung over their shoulders. James kicked a loose stone, watching it skitter into the grass.

Edward adjusted his bag, the leather strap creaking. "So, what's your grand plan then?"

"Haven't got one." James shifted his own load, the tools inside clanking. "I need a bed for the night first. The rest will sort itself after."

"Don't be daft." Edward stopped walking, forcing James to halt too. "Mary's made up the spare room before, she can do it again."

James shook his head, continuing his stride. "Your cottage barely fits you three as it is."

"Four soon enough." Edward jogged to catch up, grinning despite everything. "Mary's expecting."

"All the more reason I won't impose." James ducked under a low-hanging branch. "The Crown and Rose has decent rooms. I might hear something useful there too."

"Ah yes, nothing like drunk lords spilling their servants' secrets." Edward mimed holding a wine glass with his pinky extended. "'I say, Worthington, my stable master's run off with the cook. Simply cannot find good help these days.'"

James snorted, the first real laugh he'd managed since morning. "That's a terrible impression."

"Should've seen me in the village play last Christmas. I made a splendid duchess."

They reached the fork in the road where their paths would split. Edward scratched his chin, suddenly serious. "It's not right, you know. Them treating us like we're nothing more than tools to be discarded."

"That's exactly what we are to them." James adjusted his bag again. "Lord Ashworth probably spends more on his hunting dogs than our yearly wages combined."

"Bet his dogs can't muck out a stable though." Edward raised an eyebrow. "Or fix a broken wagon wheel in the middle of a storm."

"No, but they can sit pretty and follow commands." James smiled wryly. "Which is all they really want, isn't it?"

Edward kicked at the dirt. "Remember old Barnie, he worked that farm for thirty years, then got tossed out when a new owner wanted younger men."

"Ended up sweeping streets in London, didn't he?"

"Until the consumption got him." Edward shook his head. "That's not going to be us, Jimmy. We're better than that."

James looked down the road leading to town, where lights were beginning to flicker in windows. "Maybe. But first, I need a drink and a bed."

"Last chance for Mary's cooking instead." Edward waggled his eyebrows. "She's making her famous shepherd's pie."

"The one that nearly killed your cousin at Christmas?"

"He was drunk already. Probably would've choked on air that night." Edward laughed, then sobered. "You're sure about this?"

James nodded, already stepping toward town. "I'll be fine. Besides, someone needs to keep an eye on those fancy lords and their loose tongues."

"Just don't get too fancy yourself." Edward called after him. "Wouldn't want you developing a taste for wine and pheasant!"

"I'll try to resist!" James shouted back, waving without turning.

He heard Edward's footsteps heading the other way, toward home and family and warmth. James squared his shoulders and kept walking toward town. The Crown and Rose's windows glowed invitingly ahead, and inside, he knew, someone would need a new worker soon enough. They always did.

James pushed open the heavy wooden door of

the Crown and Rose, the familiar scent of ale and wood polish greeting him. A few regulars hunched over their drinks at scattered tables, while Florence, the barmaid, polished glasses behind the counter. Her face brightened when she spotted him.

"James Brown, as I live and breathe!" She set down her cloth, propping her elbows on the bar. "I was beginning to think you'd forgotten about us common folk."

James dropped his bag by a stool and settled onto it, "Work keeps me busy, Florence. You know how it is."

"Too busy to share a drink with old friends?" She reached for a clean glass. "The usual?"

"Better make it something stronger today."

Florence's hands stilled on the bottle she'd grabbed. "That bad, eh?"

"Patterson sold the farm." James traced a knot in the wooden counter. "The new owner's turning it into a hunting ground."

"Lord Ashworth?" Florence's eyes widened. At James's nod, she cursed under her breath. "That man's bought half the county by now. When do you leave?"

"Already have." James gestured to his bag. "Need a room for the night, if you've got one."

A FAMILY'S FIGHT FOR SURVIVAL

Florence poured him a generous measure of whiskey, sliding it across the counter. "On the house. And of course we've got a room." She leaned forward, lowering her voice. "But you might not need it."

James raised an eyebrow, taking a sip. The whiskey burned pleasantly down his throat.

"Mr. Green was in here not an hour ago." Florence wiped imaginary spots from the counter. "Looking for help on his farm. Said his eldest took ill recently, and they're short-handed with the harvest coming."

"The Green farm?" James had passed it a few times, a modest spread on the outskirts of town. "Thought they were struggling."

"They are." Florence refilled his glass without asking. "Can't offer much coin up front, but there's room and board, and proper pay once they sell their pigs at market."

James swirled the amber liquid in his glass. "Honest folk?"

"The best." Florence nodded emphatically. "Two daughters, both hard workers. Mr. Green's quiet sort, but fair. Lost his wife years back, poor man."

James took another sip, considering. "Where's the farm exactly?"

Florence grabbed a cloth and began wiping down the bar again. "Take the north road past Miller's Creek. First farm on your left after the big oak. Can't miss it - there's a red gate that needs a fresh coat of paint something fierce."

"Sounds like everything there needs work."

"Probably why they need the help." Florence grinned. "But they're good people, James. Might be just what you're looking for."

James drained his glass and stood, reaching for his coin purse.

Florence waved him off. "Those drinks were on me. But you owe me a proper visit once you're settled."

"If I get the position."

"You will." Florence grabbed a bottle of cool cider and pressed it into his hands. "For the road. It's a fair walk, and the day's still warm."

James tucked the bottle into his bag. "Thanks, Florence."

"Off with you then." She shooed him toward the door. "And James? Don't be a stranger this time."

He tipped his hat to her and stepped back into the late afternoon sun, his feet already turning toward the north road. The cider bottle clinked against his tools as he walked, a reminder that perhaps his luck hadn't completely run out after all.

James adjusted his bag on his shoulder as he approached the red gate. The paint peeled in long strips, revealing graying wood underneath. He pushed it open, wincing at the loud creak it made.

The path wound through an overgrown field, leading to a modest farmhouse with smoke curling from its chimney. A large barn loomed to the side, and from it came the unmistakable sounds of distress - both human and porcine.

"Get back here, you blasted-" A man's voice cut through the air, followed by the squealing of pigs.

James dropped his bag by the fence and jogged toward the commotion. Inside the barn, he found an older man struggling to corral three escaped pigs, who seemed determined to dash in opposite directions.

Without hesitation, James positioned himself by the open pen gate. "I'll block them here, sir!"

Mr. Green - James assumed by Florence's description - startled at his voice but recovered quickly. "Get that big one first!" He pointed to a particularly enthusiastic escapee.

James herded the first pig toward the pen, using

his body to guide rather than chase. The animal snorted but complied, trotting through the gate. The other two followed with some strategic maneuvering.

Mr. Green latched the gate firmly, panting. "Much obliged, young man. Though I don't recall hiring any help yet."

"James Brown, sir." James extended his hand. "I heard in town you might be looking for a farmhand."

Mr. Green wiped his palms on his trousers before shaking James's hand. His grip was firm despite his apparent exhaustion. "Word travels fast. You've worked farms before?"

"Six years at Patterson's place, until today." James gestured to the pen. "Dealt with my share of stubborn pigs."

"Patterson's?" Mr. Green's eyes narrowed. "Heard Lord Ashworth bought that land."

"He did. This morning, in fact." James kept his voice neutral. "We were told to clear out by sundown."

Mr. Green leaned against the pen, studying James. "I can't offer much. Times are lean, and payment would have to wait until after market."

"Florence mentioned as much. Room and board for now?"

"Small room out back." Mr. Green pointed

through the barn's open door to a modest outbuilding. "Two meals a day - breakfast and dinner. Work starts at dawn."

James nodded. "That suits me fine, sir."

"A week's trial," Mr. Green said firmly. "We'll see how you manage."

"Fair enough."

Mr. Green gestured for James to follow him. They crossed the yard to the outbuilding, which stood separate from the main house. Inside, a narrow bed occupied one wall, with a small table and chair beneath a window. A hook on the wall served as a wardrobe.

"It's not much," Mr. Green said, lighting a lamp. "But it's dry and warm enough."

"It's perfect, thank you." James set his bag on the bed. "When would you like me to start?"

"Get settled tonight. We begin at first light." Mr. Green paused at the door. "Breakfast is at six sharp. Don't be late - my daughter Iris runs a tight kitchen."

"I'll be there, sir."

Mr. Green nodded once. "Get some rest, James. Tomorrow will come soon enough."

The door closed behind him, leaving James alone in his new quarters. He sat on the bed, testing its firmness. Not the finest accommodation he'd known, but far from the worst. The mattress creaked as he lay back, staring at the ceiling.

It wasn't what he'd planned for his life, but it was a start. And sometimes, James thought as he closed his eyes, that's all a man needed.

CHAPTER 3

CHAPTER 3

Iris's eyes fluttered open to the familiar ache in her chest. The morning light came in through her thin curtains as she pushed herself up, holding her breathing to avoid another coughing fit. Her muscles protested, but she swung her legs over the bed anyway.

She pulled on her worn cotton dress, her fingers fumbling with the buttons as another cough rattled through her. The wooden stairs creaked under her feet as she made her way to the kitchen, gripping the bannister tighter than usual.

"What do you think you're doing?" Her sister stood in the doorway, hands planted firmly on her hips, looking far too authoritative for a twelve-year-old.

Iris reached for the kettle. "Making breakfast, what does it look like?"

"No, you're not." Anna darted forward, snatching the kettle from her grasp. "Doctor Morrison said bed rest. This isn't bed rest."

"It's been a week, Anna." Iris dropped into a kitchen chair, suppressing another cough. "My body isn't meant for lying about all day like some invalid."

Anna busied herself with the stove, "Well, you'll have to get used to it. Besides, I've got breakfast under control. I always do."

"Since when did you become so bossy?" Iris watched her sister crack eggs into a bowl.

"Since you decided to frighten us half to death by collapsing." Anna's voice wavered slightly. "Oh! And Father hired someone last night. A farm hand. He'll be joining us for breakfast."

Iris's stomach clenched. "He what?"

"Hired help. Finally." Anna glanced over her shoulder. "You're awfully quiet about this."

"What is there to say?" Iris stared at her hands

folded in her lap. The same hands that had managed the farm since she was ten, the same hands now deemed too weak to even crack an egg. "I suppose it had to happen eventually."

Henry Green's face softened at the sight of his eldest daughter. "How are you feeling this morning, dear?"

"Much better." Iris straightened in her chair. "I would have managed breakfast if Anna hadn't—"

"Thank goodness she did." Henry pulled out a chair, the legs scraping against the floor. "The doctor was quite clear, Iris. Four weeks minimum."

"Four weeks?" Iris's voice cracked. "But the harvest—"

"Will get done without you killing yourself over it." Henry's tone left no room for argument. "That's why we have help now."

"I'm not an invalid," Iris muttered, but another cough betrayed her words.

Anna set a cup of tea in front of her. "No, you're not. You're just someone who needs to rest before she ends up in an early grave."

"Anna!" Henry admonished, but Iris saw the fear behind her sister's sharp words.

The kitchen fell silent except for the sizzle of

eggs in the pan and the occasional clink of Anna's spoon against the pot. Iris wrapped her hands around the warm teacup, trying to ignore her father's concerned gaze and the hollow feeling in her chest that had nothing to do with her cough.

Iris perched on the windowsill of her bedroom after breakfast, a quilt wrapped around her shoulders. The morning dew still clung to the grass, but their new farmhand had already been up for hours. She watched as James hauled wooden posts across the pig pen, his shirtsleeves rolled up to reveal tanned forearms.

He paused to wipe his brow, and Iris caught herself studying the way his shoulders moved under his shirt. She shook her head, irritated at her own distraction.

The door opened behind her. "Your medicine, sister dear." Anna bustled in, carrying a tray with a glass of water. She set it down on the bedside table and followed Iris's gaze out the window. "Oh! Admiring the view, are we?"

"Don't be ridiculous." Iris turned away from the window, but not before she saw James lift a post with one hand while hammering with the other. "I'm merely checking that he's doing things properly."

"Mm-hmm." Anna perched on the bed, swinging

her legs. "He's already fixed the chicken coop, mended three fence posts, and cleared out the pig pen. Father says he's never seen anyone work so fast."

Iris's throat tightened. "I suppose I'm easily replaced then."

"That's not what I meant." Anna handed her the first medicine bottle. "He's helping, not replacing. There's a difference."

Iris swallowed the bitter liquid, grimacing. "Did he at least come in for breakfast later?"

"No, he insisted on starting work first. I took him some bread and eggs." Anna's eyes sparkled. "He was ever so grateful. Such nice manners for a farmhand."

"If you're quite finished singing his praises..." Iris reached for the second bottle.

"You know," Anna picked at a loose thread on the quilt, "with James here to help, you could finally take that secretary course you've been eyeing in the newspaper."

Iris's hand stilled. "That was just a silly dream."

"Why? You're the smartest person I know." Anna stood and straightened her apron. "And now you won't have to worry about the farm every second of every day."

"This is all I know how to do, Anna." Iris's voice came out small. "What if—"

"What if nothing." Anna took the empty medicine bottles and arranged them on the tray. "You've spent years taking care of everyone else. Maybe it's time someone took care of you."

Through the window, James laughed as he chatted with their father. Iris pressed her fingers against the glass. "I don't know how to do that."

"Then it's about time you learned." Anna squeezed her shoulder. "Besides, I've seen how you look at those course advertisements. Your hands were meant for more than just calluses."

"I don't mean to sound so ungrateful." Iris turned from the window. "It's just..."

"Strange? Different? Scary?" Anna picked up the tray. "All of the above?"

"Something like that." Iris managed a small smile.

"Well, good thing you have me to knock some sense into you." Anna headed for the door. "Now, rest. Doctor's orders. And try not to spend all day staring at our new farmhand."

"I wasn't—" Iris started, but Anna had already closed the door, her giggles echoing down the hallway.

Iris thumbed through the leather-bound book

Mrs. lucy had brought her. The words swam before her eyes as she shifted against her pillows for the tenth time. She snapped the book shut and tossed it aside.

"This is ridiculous." She swung her legs over the bed and pulled on her boots. She'd nearly made it to the door when Anna's voice rang out from the kitchen.

"And where do you think you're going?"

Iris turned to find her sister, hands covered in flour, standing in the doorway. "For a walk."

"Absolutely not." Anna wiped her hands on her apron. "Doctor Morrison said—"

"Doctor Morrison said bed rest, yes, I know." Iris reached for her shawl. "But I'm not planning to plow a field or wrangle cattle. I'm going for a walk."

"But—"

"I'll stay close to the house." Iris wrapped the shawl around her shoulders. "I just need to stretch my legs before I lose my mind entirely."

Anna's face scrunched up in worry. "Promise you won't do anything strenuous?"

"Cross my heart." Iris drew an X over her chest. "Just a short walk to clear my head."

The morning air filled her lungs as she stepped outside. She walked toward the pig pen, her feet following the familiar path without thought. The sight that greeted her made her stop short.

The pen had been completely transformed. Fresh straw covered the ground in neat layers. The feeding troughs gleamed, scrubbed clean. Even the fence posts stood straighter, reinforced with new wood.

Iris knelt beside the pen, reaching through to scratch behind Betty's ears. The pregnant sow grunted contentedly.

"How are you, old girl?" Iris murmured. "Being well taken care of, I see."

"Miss Green?"

Iris startled, losing her balance. A strong hand caught her elbow, before she could fall.

"I'm sorry." James quickly withdrew his hand. "I didn't mean to frighten you."

Iris straightened her skirts. "Mr. Brown, I presume?"

He nodded, pushing his cap back. "James Brown, miss. Though most folks call me Jimmy."

"Iris Green." She gestured to the pen. "I see you've been busy."

"Just trying to get things sorted." He shifted his weight. "Though, begging your pardon, miss, but shouldn't you be resting? Your father mentioned you've been unwell."

Iris's spine stiffened. "I'm perfectly capable of standing in my own yard, Mr. Brown."

"Of course." His ears reddened. "I didn't mean to imply—that is—are you feeling better?"

The genuine concern in his voice softened her irritation. "Yes, thank you. Though everyone seems determined to treat me like spun glass."

"Can't blame them for worrying." James leaned against the fence post. "Your sister told me about your collapse."

"Did she now?" Iris made a mental note to have a word with Anna about gossiping with farmhands.

"She's quite protective of you." A smile tugged at his mouth. "Gave me strict instructions about not letting you anywhere near the heavy work when you're better."

"Did she also tell you I've managed this farm since I was ten?"

"She did." James nodded. "Said you're the hardest worker she's ever known. Makes me wonder if I'll measure up."

Iris glanced around the immaculate pig pen.

Iris studied the new feeding setup in the pig pen, her fingers drumming against the fence post. The troughs had been arranged in a completely different pattern than her usual method, with dividers she'd never seen before.

"What's all this then?" She gestured at the setup.

James straightened. "I've sectioned off the feeding areas. Makes it easier to—"

"We've always fed them together." Iris stepped closer to the fence. "The arrangement worked perfectly fine before."

"With respect, Miss Green, this way ensures each pig gets their fair share." James picked up a bucket and demonstrated how the feed would flow through the new dividers. "See here? The slower eaters won't get bullied out of their portion."

Iris watched Betty nudge one of the dividers with her snout. "They've managed well enough until now."

"I noticed some of the younger ones were a bit thin." James set the bucket down, wiping his hands on his trousers. "On my last farm, we found this method helped them all maintain proper weight, especially the pregnant sows."

"Hmm." Iris crossed her arms, hating how logical his explanation sounded.

"We had over five hundred pigs to manage there." James leaned against the fence post, careful to keep a respectful distance. "When you're handling that many, you learn a few tricks to make sure none go hungry."

"Five hundred?" Despite herself, Iris's eyebrows rose. "Where was this?"

"Thornfield Farm." James adjusted his cap. "Spent six years there before..." He trailed off, something flickering across his face. "Well, before circumstances changed."

Iris felt her curiosity pique, but she swallowed her questions. "I should return to the house. Anna will send out a search party if I'm gone too long."

"Of course." James stepped back, giving her space to turn. "Though, Miss Green?"

She paused. "Yes?"

"I know you've built something special here." His voice was gentle. "I'm not trying to change that. Just hoping to help where I can."

Iris nodded stiffly and walked away. Her chest burned, and not from her cough this time. She'd managed those pigs since they were piglets, knew each one's quirks and habits. And here was this stranger, with his clever ideas and reasonable explanations, making her feel like...

Like what? Like she'd done it wrong all these years?

No, that wasn't it. She stopped at the garden gate,

watching a sparrow hop along the fence. The truth was his method probably would work better. She'd seen how Martha, the smallest of last spring's litter, always got pushed aside at feeding time. The dividers would solve that problem neatly.

Iris paused at the kitchen door, her hand on the latch. Why did his competence irritate her so? He'd done nothing but help, yet each improvement felt like a personal slight.

The door swung open before she could turn the handle. Anna stood there, flour still dusting her apron. "Done supervising already?"

"I wasn't supervising." Iris brushed past her sister. "I was taking a walk."

"That just happened to lead you to where James was working?"

"Don't you have bread to bake?" Iris sank into a kitchen chair, suddenly tired.

"It's in the oven." Anna poured her a glass of water. "So, what do you think of his improvements?"

Iris took a sip, avoiding her sister's gaze. "They're... efficient."

"High praise indeed." Anna laughed. "Coming from you, that's practically a declaration of undying gratitude."

"I'm going back to bed." Iris pushed herself up from the chair.

"Because you're tired, or because you don't want to admit he might actually know what he's doing?"

Iris paused at the bottom of the stairs. "Because Doctor Morrison said bed rest, and for once, I'm going to do as I'm told."

CHAPTER 4

CHAPTER 4

James wiped the sweat from his brow as he hauled fresh feed to the pig pen. The morning sun had barely crested the horizon, but the air already held that sticky warmth that promised a scorching day ahead. He'd gotten an early start, determined to prove his worth during this trial week.

The crunch of boots on gravel made him turn. Iris Green approached, her face pale but set with stubborn resolve. She carried a smaller feed bucket, its weight making her list slightly to one side.

"Miss Green." He straightened, setting down his own bucket. "Should you be out here?"

"I'm perfectly capable of feeding my own pigs, Mr. Brown." She moved past him toward the pen gate.

James stepped in front of her. "With all due respect, you collapsed two days ago. Your sister mentioned the doctor ordered rest."

"Did he now?" Iris's green eyes flashed. "And I suppose you and Anna have been discussing my condition at length?"

"Only insofar as it affects the running of the farm." He kept his voice steady, reasonable. "Please, let me handle this. You're welcome to supervise if you'd like."

She clutched the bucket tighter. "I don't need supervision in my own pig pen."

"No, but I might." He offered a small smile. "I'm still learning your methods."

"Your methods seemed perfectly adequate yesterday." The words carried a sharp edge.

James sighed, reaching for her bucket. "Miss Green, please. You're still recovering."

She yanked it away, sloshing feed onto her boots. "I've managed these pigs through far worse than a simple cold."

"And now you don't have to." He met her gaze directly. "That's why your father hired me."

"To replace me?"

"To help you."

Iris set the bucket down with more force than necessary. "Well then, by all means, help away. Show me how they do things at the grand Thornfield Farm."

James began distributing feed among the troughs, conscious of her critical gaze. When he reached the pregnant sows' pen, she clicked her tongue.

"You're giving them too much. They'll get fat and have trouble farrowing."

He continued measuring carefully. "These portions are calculated based on their weight and stage of pregnancy."

"We've never needed fancy calculations here." She crossed her arms. "Our way has worked fine."

James straightened, patience wearing thin. "Is that why you're selling off stock? Because everything's working so well?"

The moment the words left his mouth, he knew he'd gone too far. Iris's face went white, then red.

"How dare you—"

"I apologize." He held up a hand. "That was out of

line. But Miss Green, do you want to know what I think?"

"Not particularly."

"I think you'd rather see this farm struggle than accept help from an outsider." He met her furious gaze. "And that's not fair to your father or your sister."

"You know nothing about my family or this farm." Her voice shook. "Nothing."

"I know hard times when I see them." He softened his tone. "And I know pride can be expensive."

Iris's hands clenched into fists. Without another word, she turned on her heel and stormed away, leaving James alone with the squealing pigs and words he couldn't take back.

James watched Iris's retreating form until she disappeared around the corner of the house. He shook his head and returned to distributing feed. The pigs crowded the troughs, with their enthusiastic grunts.

"Mr. Brown?" Anna called from behind him.

He turned to find her balancing a wooden tray loaded with bread, cheese, and what smelled like fresh coffee. She walked carefully between the muddy patches, her oversized boots making the task more difficult.

"Here, let me help you with that." James took the tray from her hands.

"I thought you might like some breakfast." Anna brushed her hands on her apron. "And... I saw Iris storm inside. She looked rather cross."

James set the tray on a nearby fence post. "Your sister and I had a difference of opinion about pig feed portions."

"She's not usually so..." Anna wrinkled her nose, searching for the right word. "Difficult."

"I'd be surprised if she was." James tore off a piece of bread and popped it in his mouth. "This is excellent, by the way."

Anna beamed. "I made it myself. Well, mostly myself. Father had to help with the oven." She kicked at a clump of dirt. "I'm sorry about Iris. She's just... this farm is everything to her. Has been since Mother died."

James poured coffee into the tin cup Anna had brought. "How old was she?"

"Ten when Mother passed. I was three." Anna leaned against the fence post. "She took over everything - the house, the farm accounts, looking after me. Father was... well, he needed time."

"That's a lot of responsibility for a young girl."

James watched a pair of piglets chase each other around their mother.

"And now she can't do any of it because she's ill." Anna picked at a loose thread on her sleeve. "I think it's driving her mad, watching someone else handle her tasks."

James nodded. "I'd feel the same way. When you've built something with your own hands, watching another person change it..." He took a sip of coffee. "Well, it's like watching someone rearrange your bones."

"That's a peculiar way of putting it." Anna wrinkled her nose.

"But accurate, I'd wager." James smiled. "Don't worry about your sister's reaction. I expected it."

"You did?"

"Of course. Pride's a funny thing, Miss Anna. Sometimes it's all we have left when times get hard."

Anna considered this, her young face serious. "Will you stay? Even if Iris continues to be... difficult?"

James set down his cup. "I've weathered worse storms than your sister's temper. Besides," he gestured to the pen where the pigs contentedly gorged themselves, "these fellows need me."

James watched Anna's shoulders slump as she

picked up a stray piece of straw, twisting it between her fingers. Her usual brightness dimmed.

"I'm scared she won't get better," Anna's voice cracked. "I hear her coughing at night."

James set down his coffee cup and adjusted a loose board on the fence. "Your sister strikes me as the type who'd outrun a hurricane if she set her mind to it."

"You've only known her three days." Anna kicked at a clump of hay.

"Long enough to see she's tougher than most." He hammered the board into place with the heel of his hand. "Some people are like oak trees - they bend in the storm, but they don't break."

Anna brightened slightly. "She is rather stubborn."

"Stubborn people make the best survivors." James collected the empty feed buckets. "Trust me on that."

"I suppose... You know, you should join us for dinner tonight."

James paused mid-scratch. "I wouldn't want to impose."

"Didn't Father tell you to come for meals?" Anna's eyebrows shot up.

"Well, yes, but-"

"Then you're coming." She pointed a brush at

him. "And maybe... maybe tell Iris she could sit with you while you work sometimes? So she feels useful?"

James considered this as he shooed away a particularly enthusiastic piglet from investigating his boots. "That's not a bad idea."

"She'd never admit it, but she hates being stuck inside." Anna lowered her voice. "And she keeps watching you from the window."

"Does she now?" James fought back a smile.

"Oh yes. Pretends she's not, but I've caught her." Anna grinned. "So, you'll come to dinner?"

"If you're certain it won't be an intrusion."

Anna rolled her eyes. "You're being silly. From now on, you eat with us. No arguments."

"Yes, ma'am." James gave her a mock salute.

"Good." Anna handed back the brush. "Now I'd better go check on Father before he burns the porridge again."

* * *

JAMES STRAIGHTENED his collar and brushed off his work clothes before knocking on the Green's front door. The evening air had cooled, bringing relief after the day's heat. His knuckles had barely touched the wood when Anna yanked the door open.

"You came!" She bounced on her toes. "Come in, come in. Everyone's already at the table."

James followed her through the narrow hallway, ducking slightly under the low beams. The house smelled of fresh bread and something savory that made his stomach growl.

Anna gestured to an empty chair beside Iris. "Sit here, Mr. Brown."

Iris kept her eyes fixed on her plate as James settled into the chair. Mr. Green nodded a greeting from the head of the table, while Anna bustled around, ladling steaming stew into bowls.

"How are those pigs settling in with the new feeding schedule?" Mr. Green spooned sugar into his tea, the spoon clinking against the china.

James accepted a bowl from Anna. "Very well, sir. The pregnant sows especially are responding to the measured portions."

"Good, good." Mr. Green tore off a chunk of bread. "And the fencing in the north field?"

"Repaired all the loose posts today." James reached for the salt, his arm briefly brushing Iris's. She shifted away slightly. "Though we might want to consider replacing that whole section come spring."

"Hmm, lets hope for better days by spring," Mr. Green set down his spoon. "I've been thinking about planting turnips in the lower field. Early variety could do well there."

"The soil's perfect for it." James nodded. "We had good luck with turnips at Thornfield. I can help with the planting when you're ready."

Iris's fork scraped against her plate. "We've never planted turnips in that field."

"No time like the present to try something new." Mr. Green smiled at his daughter. "James here has experience with crop rotation. Might do the soil some good."

"I could show you the methods we used," James offered, glancing at Iris. "If you're interested."

She pushed a potato around her plate. "I suppose we could discuss it."

"Excellent!" Anna clapped her hands. "And I can help too. I'm quite good at digging holes."

"You're quite good at making holes in your stockings," Iris muttered, but James caught the hint of a smile.

"The turnips will need proper spacing," James explained, drawing an invisible pattern on the tablecloth. "But with all of us working together, we could have them in the ground before the frost breaks."

Mr. Green nodded approvingly. "It's settled then. We'll start preparing the field next week."

"Could we plant some flowers too?" Anna asked, refilling water glasses. "Just along the edges?"

"Flowers don't feed people, Anna," Iris sighed.

"But they feed the soul," James found himself saying. "And they attract beneficial insects for the crops."

Iris looked at him then, really looked at him, for the first time that evening. "You know about companion planting?"

"I learned it from my mother." James met her gaze. "She always said a farm needs both beauty and function to thrive."

"She sounds wise," Mr. Green said.

"She was." James turned his attention back to his stew, the old grief a familiar weight.

Anna touched his shoulder as she cleared empty bowls. "Well, I think turnips and flowers sound perfect together."

After dinner, James helped Anna clear the dishes while Iris dabbed at the tablecloth where her father had spilled his tea. Mr. Green pushed back his chair.

"Well, I'll be turning in. Good night, all." He patted Iris's shoulder as he passed.

Before Iris could follow suit, James set down the stack of plates. "Miss Green, might I have a word?"

She paused halfway out of her chair. "I should help Anna with-"

"Go on," Anna called from the kitchen. "I've got these."

James gestured toward the living room. "It won't take long."

Iris smoothed her skirts and led the way. The living room held a worn settee, two armchairs, and a small fireplace where embers still glowed. She perched on the edge of the settee while James remained standing, hands clasped behind his back.

"About this morning," he began, "I spoke out of turn."

"You did." Iris twisted a loose thread from her sleeve.

"The thing is," James turned to face her, "I know what it's like to lose something you've built. When Thornfield was sold..." He shook his head. "Well, I didn't handle it gracefully."

"You think that's what this is about?" Iris stood, straightening to her full height. "That I'm afraid of losing the farm?"

"Aren't you?"

She crossed to the fireplace, prodding the embers with the poker. "Of course, I am. But that's not why-"

She set the poker down with a clang. "I don't mean to be difficult. Or rude. It's just..."

"Everything's changing." James moved closer, careful to maintain a proper distance. "And you feel powerless to stop it."

"Yes." She wrapped her arms around herself. "And now I can't even feed the pigs properly."

"About that." James leaned against the mantel. "I have a proposition."

Iris raised an eyebrow. "Oh?"

"Come to the pens each morning. Watch what I'm doing, tell me if you think I'm making mistakes." He held up a hand as she opened her mouth. "But you have to promise to actually listen when I explain my methods."

"And if I disagree?"

"Then we'll discuss it. Like reasonable adults." He smiled. "Though I warn you, I can be rather stubborn."

A laugh escaped her. "More stubborn than me?"

"We'll have to see, won't we?"

Iris turned to face him fully. "And you'll actually consider my suggestions?"

"As long as you promise to respect my experience as well." James met her gaze steadily. "Deal?"

She drew herself up. "Well, I suppose I could-"

"Ah," James held up a finger. "You promised."

Iris's mouth dropped open, then curved into a genuine smile. "I did no such thing! I was about to-"

"Promise?" James grinned.

She laughed again, the sound warming the room more than any fire could. "Very well, Mr. Brown. You have my word."

"James."

"What?"

"If we're going to be pig-feeding partners, you might as well call me James."

Iris tucked a loose strand of hair behind her ear. "James, then." She glanced toward the kitchen where Anna hummed as she worked. "I should help her finish up."

"Of course." James stepped back, allowing her to pass. At the doorway, she paused.

"Thank you,"

CHAPTER 5

CHAPTER 5

"Come on, Bessie, just a few more bites." Iris held out an apple slice to the heavily pregnant sow, who snuffled at it with disinterest. The sun casted zebra-like stripes across the hay-strewn floor. After a week of observing James's methods, she'd grown accustomed to the new feeding schedule, though she still insisted on checking on the animals herself.

Bessie shifted uncomfortably, her swollen belly nearly dragging on the ground. Something about her movement caught Iris's attention.

"You're not just being stubborn today, are you?"

Iris set down the feeding bucket and crouched beside the pen. Bessie let out a low grunt, different from her usual sounds. The sow's sides heaved, and she began pawing at the hay.

Iris's heart jumped. "Oh Lord, it's happening now." She hitched up her skirts and scrambled to her feet. "James! James, come quickly!"

She heard the thud of boots on packed earth before James appeared around the corner of the barn, his shirt sleeves rolled up and hair tousled from work.

"What's wrong?"

"It's Bessie, she's starting."

James jumped over the low fence and was beside her in seconds, assessing the situation. "How long has she been like this?"

"Just started. She wouldn't eat her breakfast, and then—" Bessie let out another grunt, more insistent this time.

"Right then." James shed his outer shirt, leaving him in his work shirt. "We'll need clean straw, hot water, and rags. Lots of rags."

Iris nodded, already moving. "I'll fetch Anna…"

"No time. She's progressing fast." James's voice was calm but firm. "I need you here."

Iris hesitated for a split second, then nodded.

She'd helped birth piglets before, but always with her father's guidance. This would be different.

"The supplies are in the barn," she said, moving quickly. "I'll be right back."

When she returned with an armful of fresh straw and rags, James had already cleared space around Bessie, who was now lying on her side.

"Here," James said, taking some of the rags. "We need to keep her calm."

Iris knelt beside him, her skirts already gathering dirt. "Bessie, good girl," she murmured, stroking the sow's heaving flank. "We're right here."

"She trusts you," James observed, positioning himself at Bessie's rear. "So, keep talking to her."

The next few minutes passed, and Bessie's grunts grew more frequent. Iris could see the sow's muscles contracting.

"I can see the first one," James announced. "Iris, I need you to hold her."

Iris moved to Bessie's head, continuing to stroke and soothe her. The sow pushed, and James's hands helped her.

"There we go," he said softly, and a moment later, a tiny piglet slid into the world. James quickly cleared its airways and placed it near Bessie's warm belly.

"One down," Iris said, unable to keep the smile from her voice.

"There are still more coming," James warned, and sure enough, Bessie began pushing again.

They worked together, James delivered each piglet while Iris kept Bessie calm and helped clean the newborns. The morning sun climbed higher as one piglet became two, then four, then six.

"Last one, I think," James said, his forearms slick with birthing fluid. "She's doing brilliantly."

Iris watched in fascination as the final piglet emerged. This one was smaller than the others, and for a heart-stopping moment, it didn't move.

"James—"

"I see it." He quickly rubbed the tiny creature with a clean rag, stimulating its breathing. After what felt like an eternity, the piglet gave a weak squeak and began to wiggle.

"Oh, thank goodness." Iris helped guide the runt to join its siblings at Bessie's belly.

James sat back on his heels, wiping his brow with his sleeve. "Seven healthy piglets. That's a fine litter."

Iris looked at him properly for the first time since he'd arrived at her call. His shirt was soaked with sweat and other fluids, his hair was a complete mess, and there was dirt streaked across his cheek. She probably looked just as disheveled.

"We did it," she said, then corrected herself. "You did it."

James shook his head. "We did it together. I couldn't have managed without you keeping her calm." He gave her a warm smile that made something flutter in her chest. "You're good with them. The animals, I mean."

"I should be. I've spent enough time with them." Iris watched the piglets nursing, already competing for the best positions. "Though I have to admit, your methods have made things easier this past week."

"High praise indeed from Miss Green," James teased, standing and offering her his hand.

Iris took it, allowing him to help her up. His hand was warm and calloused, and he held on perhaps a moment longer than necessary before letting go.

"We should clean up," she said, suddenly aware of her own state. "Anna will have a fit if I track this mess into the house."

Iris wiped her hands on a relatively clean patch of her apron while James gathered the soiled rags.

"We should get these cleaned before—"

The crunch of boots on gravel made her turn. A tall man in an immaculate black suit stood at the pen's entrance, his nose wrinkled at the scene before him. His polished walking stick gleamed in the sunlight.

"Miss Green?" He removed his hat, revealing carefully styled dark hair. "I am William Wood."

Iris smoothed her skirts uselessly, painfully aware of the state of her appearance. "Mr. Wood. What brings you to our farm?"

"I had hoped to speak with you." His eyes flicked to James, who was still collecting the birthing supplies. "In private, if you please."

"Whatever you have to say, you can say it in front of Mr. Brown." Iris crossed her arms. "He works here."

William's lip curled. "In your current... condition?"

"We've just delivered seven piglets," Iris gestured to Bessie and her nursing babies. "If our appearance offends you, perhaps you should have sent word of your visit."

William cleared his throat, straightening his already rigid posture. "Very well. Miss Green, I've come to make you an offer. I wish to court you."

Iris blinked. "I beg your pardon?"

"My father owns the largest grain mill in the county. We've noticed your farm's potential, and with proper management—" He paused, looking pointedly at James. "Well, a marriage between us would be advantageous for both parties."

Iris felt her cheeks heat. "Mr. Wood—"

"You would want for nothing," he continued, taking a step forward. "No more manual labor. No more..." He gestured at their surroundings. "This."

James shifted beside her, and Iris felt rather than saw his tension.

"Mr. Wood," Iris kept her voice level. "While I appreciate your... offer, I must decline."

William's face darkened. "You cannot be serious."

"I am quite serious."

"Do you understand what I'm offering? Security. Position. A proper life, not this—" He jabbed his walking stick at the pig pen. "—this squalor."

"This 'squalor' is my home," Iris took a step forward, her hands balling into fists. "And I won't have you insulting it."

"You're making a grave mistake." William's voice rose. "A woman in your position—"

"My position is exactly where I choose to be." Iris cut him off. "Now, if you'll excuse us, we have work to do."

William's face contorted. "Your father will hear about this."

"I'm sure he will." Iris turned her back on him, her heart pounding. "Good day, Mr. Wood."

She heard him sputter, followed by the angry retreat. Only when the sound had faded did she let out a shaky breath.

"Are you alright?" James asked quietly.

Iris nodded, though her hands trembled. "I should go in." She walked quickly toward the house.

Iris pushed open the kitchen door, her skirts heavy with mud and worse. Anna sat at the table, peeling potatoes, and looked up with wide eyes at her sister's disheveled state.

"Good Lord, what happened to you?" Anna dropped her potato and knife with a clatter.

"Bessie had her piglets." Iris couldn't keep the pride from her voice as she pumped water into the washbasin. "Seven of them, all healthy."

Anna bounced up from her chair. "Seven! Even the runt made it?"

"James saved that one." Iris scrubbed her hands, watching the water turn murky. "He knew exactly what to do when it wasn't breathing properly."

"Of course he did." Anna's tone held a teasing note that made Iris look up sharply.

"Don't start."

"I wasn't starting anything." Anna picked up her

knife again, "Though what did that fancy gentleman want? I saw him storm off like someone had insulted his mother's cooking."

Iris dried her hands on a clean cloth. "That was Mr. Wood. He came to make me an offer of marriage."

The potato Anna was holding shot out of her hands and rolled across the floor. "He what?"

"Oh yes." Iris retrieved the escaped vegetable. "He graciously offered to rescue me from our 'squalid' existence."

"No!" Anna gasped, then burst into giggles. "What did you say?"

"I told him exactly where he could put his offer." Iris dropped into a chair. "Though not in those exact words."

"And you did this while covered in pig birth?" Anna clutched her sides, practically howling now. "Oh, to have seen his face!"

"He did look rather scandalized." Iris felt her own lips twitching. "Especially when I refused to send James away for our 'private conversation.'"

"The audacity of these men!" Anna wiped tears from her eyes. "First Mr. Patterson thinking he could buy the farm for half its worth, and now this Mr. Wood assuming you'd swoon at his feet."

"At least James has some sense about him." The words slipped out before Iris could stop them.

Anna's eyebrows shot up. "Oh? And what sense would that be?"

"The farming kind," Iris said quickly, standing. "I need a bath. I smell worse than the pig pen."

"You're not wrong there." Anna wrinkled her nose. "Though I notice you didn't deny—"

"I'm going now." Iris headed for the stairs, Anna's laughter following her up.

"Don't use all the hot water!" Anna called after her. "Some of us still need to wash up before dinner!"

CHAPTER 6

James carried the lantern down the path to the pig pen later that night. The air held a crisp chill that made him pull his coat tighter. He needed to check on Bessie and her newborns one last time before turning in.

The piglets huddled close to their mother's warmth, tiny snouts nuzzling against her as they nursed. James hung the lantern on a hook and leaned over the pen's edge, counting each piglet to ensure none had wandered.

"They're quite the sight, aren't they?"

James startled, nearly dropping the small notebook he'd pulled from his pocket. He turned to find Iris standing in the doorway, a shawl wrapped around her shoulders.

"Miss Green." He straightened his posture. "I wasn't expecting anyone else out here at this hour."

"I couldn't sleep without checking on them myself." She moved closer to the pen, her steps quiet but purposeful. "The little runt seems stronger already."

"He's a fighter." James pointed to where the smallest piglet had wedged himself between his siblings. "Gets that from his mother, I'd say."

Iris leaned against the pen's edge, close enough that James caught the faint scent of lavender. "It's remarkable how protective sows are of their young. Did you know they sing to their piglets while nursing?"

"Let me guess, you read that in Whitfield's 'Animal Husbandry and Care'?"

Her eyes widened. "You know Whitfield's work?"

"I do read occasionally." James smiled, tucking his notebook away. "Though I admit, most of what I know comes from experience rather than books."

"Mrs. Lucy, our town librarian and my mother's best friend brings me new books whenever she visits." Iris's face lit up as she spoke. "She says I'm her most dedicated scholar."

"A librarian who delivers? That's quite the service."

"She's known me since I was small. She brings anything she thinks might help with the farm." Iris reached down to scratch behind Bessie's ears. "Though I suspect she also slips in a few novels when Father isn't looking."

James chuckled. "Your secret's safe with me. Though I doubt anyone would fault you for reading a bit of fiction."

"And what about you? Do you read hide any forbidden novels hidden away in that notebook of yours?"

"This is just feed calculations and pig weights, I'm afraid." He adjusted the lantern's height. "Though I did enjoy 'Pride and Prejudice' when I managed to borrow a copy last year."

"Mr. Brown!" Iris pressed a hand to her chest in mock scandal. "Reading romance novels? Whatever would the pigs think?"

"They're surprisingly good listeners." He gestured to Bessie, who had lifted her head at their conversation. "Though their literary criticism leaves something to be desired."

James watched as Iris laughed, the sound warm and infectious. It was rare to see her so at ease. He took a moment to appreciate the way her green eyes sparkled in the lantern light, then asked, "Do you love the farm?"

The question caught Iris off guard. She stopped scratching Bessie's ears and looked at James, eyebrows raised in surprise. "What do you mean?"

James shrugged, trying to seem casual. "I know you've been taking care of this place since you were young. But if you didn't have to, would you choose the farm?"

Iris stared at him, her expression unreadable. She seemed to be considering his words carefully. "I... I don't know," she finally admitted. "I've always had the farm, always needed to take care of it..."

James nodded, encouraging her to continue. "But if you had a choice – if you didn't have to take care of the farm – would you still choose this life?"

"I... I don't know. I've never let myself think about it."

"Never?"

"What's the point?" Iris looked away, her gaze drifting to the piglets once more.

"I've thought about taking a secretarial course Mrs. Lucy mentioned," she said softly. "I'd love to study, to learn something new, but who would manage things here? Father tries, but he needs help. Anna has her own dreams, and I want her to start school."

James leaned against the pen, arms crossed over his chest. "There are always options... The farm won't fall apart if you take time for yourself."

"Options?" Iris turned to face him. "Like what? Marry William Wood and become a proper lady?"

"That's not what I meant-"

"I can't choose when there's no choice to make." She wrapped her shawl tighter around her shoulders. "This farm is our livelihood. Without me here, it might fall apart."

James considered her words for a moment before speaking again. "Maybe you're right," he conceded. "But it sounds like you're not even giving yourself the chance to find out."

She opened her mouth to reply but she coughed, a harsh sound that echoed in the night.

"You're still not well," James observed with concern. "You should go inside and rest."

"I'll be fine," Iris insisted.

"No," James said firmly. "You need to take care of yourself too. Don't come out tomorrow morning; Mr. Green and I will take some pigs to sell."

Iris hesitated but finally nodded. "Alright," she agreed reluctantly.

"Goodnight then," James said with a small smile.

"Goodnight,"

* * *

JAMES AND HENRY loaded the pigs onto the cart before dawn. The pigs grunted and shuffled on the wooden planks as James secured them with ropes.

"Steady now," Henry murmured, patting one of the larger pigs on its rump. "We need to get a good price today."

James nodded, his hands moving as he tied off the last rope. "We'll do our best, Mr. Green."

They set off toward the village market, the cart creaking under the weight of their stock. James kept a steady pace, his eyes scanning the horizon as the first light of daybreak painted the sky in shades of pink and orange.

The village market was already bustling by the time they arrived. Vendors shouted out their wares, children darted between stalls, and the scent of fresh bread mingled with that of livestock. James guided the cart to their usual spot, right next to Mr. Stone's vegetable stall.

Henry jumped down first, adjusting his cap. "Let's get these pigs unloaded."

James followed suit, lifting one of the smaller pigs from the cart and placing it into a pen they'd set up for display.

As they finished setting up, James noticed a group of farmers gathered a few stalls down. One of them, a burly man with a thick mustache, caught his eye and began walking over.

"Morning, Green," the man called out as he approached. "I see you brought some pigs to market today."

"Morning, Barnaby," Henry replied tersely. "Yes, we did."

Barnaby leaned over the pen, scrutinizing the pigs with a critical eye. "These pigs don't look so good," he said loudly enough for passersby to hear. "Sickly stock if you ask me."

James felt a surge of anger. "Our pigs are healthy," he said firmly. "They're well-fed and well-cared for."

Barnaby snorted. "That's not what I heard. Word around town is that Green's farm has been struggling." He looked around at the gathering crowd. "Who knows what kind of sickness these pigs might be carrying?"

Murmurs rippled through the onlookers as Barnaby's words took root.

Henry's face flushed with frustration. "Our pigs are fine," he insisted.

James stepped forward, "We stand by our stock," he said clearly. "Anyone who buys from us will get healthy pigs."

Barnaby chuckled darkly. "We'll see about that." He turned to leave but not before casting one last glance over his shoulder at Henry and James.

Potential buyers whispered among themselves and moved on without stopping at their stall.

Henry sighed heavily as he watched them go. "This is bad," he muttered under his breath.

"We can't give up," James said resolutely. He grabbed a small piglet from their pen and held it up for everyone to see. "Look at this piglet!" he called out loudly to anyone within earshot.

A few curious faces turned towards him.

"This piglet is strong and healthy," James continued passionately as he stroked its back gently for emphasis while maintaining eye contact with those watching him intently now.

He placed it back down into its pen carefully before continuing.

"Our farm takes pride in raising quality

livestock."

Despite his efforts though, the crowd remained skeptical.

One woman shook her head dismissively. "I'm not risking my money on sick animals."

Another man said in agreeing, "Yeah."

Henry clenched his fists helplessly beside him.

"I'm sorry," Henry said quietly when most people had dispersed. "Maybe we should pack up."

James shook his head stubbornly. "Not yet. There must be someone willing."

But after hours standing under hot sun trying to convince people otherwise, they still hadn't sold single pig.

Disheartened they started packing things up again.

"This isn't right," James muttered angrily tying ropes securing pens onto cart.

"It's alright son, you tried your best... We'll find another way."

James guided the cart back through the farm gates, his shoulders tense from the long, fruitless day. The pigs grunted in the back, seemingly unaware of their rejected status at market. He jumped down from the cart and began untying the ropes while Mr. Green trudged toward the house.

"I'll get these settled back in their pen," James called after him, but Mr. Green just waved a hand without turning around.

He'd just placed the third one into the pen when quick footsteps approached behind him.

"What happened?" Iris stood at the gate, her arms crossed. "Father walked straight upstairs without a word."

James wiped his hands on his trousers. "We didn't sell a single pig."

"What? That's impossible." Iris stepped closer, her eyes narrowing. "Our pigs always sell."

"Barnaby made sure everyone thought they were diseased." James lifted another pig down, trying to keep his anger in check. "Called them sickly stock right in front of everyone."

"He what?" Iris's voice rose sharply. "That pompous-" She cut herself off, pacing along the fence. "Our pigs used to be the best in the market. Everyone knew it."

James set the last pig down and secured the gate. "I've been meaning to talk to you about that." He pulled his notebook from his pocket and flipped it open. "I've been tracking their growth. They're not gaining weight like they should."

Iris stopped pacing. "What do you mean?"

"Look." He showed her his careful notations. "A pig this age should be nearly twenty pounds heavier."

"But we're feeding them the same way we always have."

"That's the problem." James tucked the notebook away. "The old methods aren't working anymore. Other farms are using new feed mixtures, better breeding stock."

"What are you suggesting?"

"We need to change our approach." James walked to the water trough, Iris following. "There's a feed mixture I used at Thornfield. it increases their appetite, helps them put on weight faster. And if we brought in some Yorkshire boars to breed with our sows…"

"Stop." Iris held up her hand. "Do you know how much new feed and new breeding stocks would cost??"

"Yes, but-"

"Father would never agree." She shook her head. "We can barely afford our current expenses."

"Then we diversify." James turned to face her fully. "Add some dairy cows, maybe sheep. Different revenue streams mean we're not relying solely on the pigs."

"More animals means more feed, more care,

more everything." Iris ran a hand through her hair. "We don't have that kind of money."

"But if we could get a loan-"

"No." Iris's voice was firm. "Father won't take on debt. Not after..." She trailed off, looking away.

"After what?"

"It doesn't matter." She straightened her shoulders. "We'll find another way."

"Iris." James stepped closer. "The farm can't continue like this. Something has to change."

"You think I don't know that?" She gestured at the pig pen. "But we can't risk what little we have on uncertain changes."

"Sometimes the biggest risk is not taking any risk at all."

Iris looked at him for a long moment. "That's easy for you to say. This isn't your family's legacy on the line."

"No, but I care about this farm too." James met her gaze steadily. "And I care about the people on it."

A flush crept up Iris's neck. She opened her mouth to respond, but the dinner bell rang from the house.

"Anna's calling us in." She stepped back. "We should go."

CHAPTER 7

CHAPTER 7

The kitchen felt unusually quiet as Iris ladled stew into their bowls. Steam curled up from the dishes, but no one seemed interested in eating. Anna pushed her spoon through the thick broth, creating little channels that filled right back in.

Henry reached for the whiskey bottle, pouring another generous measure into his cup. His hands shook slightly as he set it down.

Iris watched her father down the long drink. That was his third glass already. Her stomach clenched as he reached for the bottle again.

"Perhaps that's enough for tonight, Father."

He set the glass down with a sharp clank. "I'll decide when I've had enough."

"I only meant—"

"I know what you meant." He took another long drink, droplets catching in his beard. "You're always telling me what to do in my own house."

Iris straightened her spine. "That's not what I'm doing. Doctor Morris said your liver—"

"Damn Doctor Morris!" His fist hit the table, making the bowls rattle. Anna flinched. "What does he know about running a farm? About providing for a family?"

"Father, please—"

"Please what?" He stood, swaying slightly. "Please pretend everything's fine. Please ignore that we're one bad season away from losing it all?"

Anna's lower lip trembled. "We're doing better now that James is here—"

"Better?" He laughed harshly. "We had to hire help because I can't manage my own land anymore. Because your sister's been sick. Because everything's falling apart!"

Tears spilled down Anna's cheeks. Iris pushed back from the table, her chair scraping against the floor. "Anna, go upstairs."

"But—"

"Now, please."

Anna fled, her footsteps thundering up the stairs. Their father reached for the bottle again.

"You think you can order everyone around?" He poured unsteadily, whiskey sloshing onto the tablecloth. "Tell your sister what to do, tell me what to do—"

"I'm trying to help!" Iris's voice cracked. "We all are. But drinking won't solve anything."

"No?" He raised the glass. "It helps me forget that I'm failing my daughters. That I can't give you the life your mother wanted for you."

"We don't need—"

"Look at you." His eyes were glassy. "Twenty years old, should be married by now. Instead, you're here, working yourself sick trying to keep this worthless farm alive."

"It's not worthless." Iris's hands clenched at her sides. "And I don't want to be married. I want to be here."

"Because you have to be."

"Because it's home!" Her voice rose despite herself. "Because we're family, and families help each other!"

He slumped back into his chair, the fight

draining from him as quickly as it had come. "Some father I turned out to be."

"Father—"

But he just shook his head, staring into his glass as if it held all the answers he couldn't find.

The kitchen fell into a heavy silence, broken only by her father's ragged breathing and the soft clink of the whiskey bottle against his glass. Iris's heart ached watching him spiral deeper into his misery. She'd seen this pattern before after her mother's death and she did not like it one bit.

"You're a coward, Mr. Green."

Iris startled violently, suddenly remembering James's was even at the table. He'd been so quiet during their argument, she'd completely forgotten he was there. "James!"

But James wasn't looking at her. His jaw was set, eyes fixed on her father with an intensity that made her breath catch.

"These girls, your daughters, are working themselves to the bone trying to keep this farm going. Iris pushes herself until she's sick, Anna's growing up too fast and taking up responsibilities far beyond her age, and what are you doing? Drowning yourself in whiskey and self-pity?"

Mr. Green's face flushed dark red. "How dare you-"

"No, sir, how dare you? ... You have two incredible daughters who love you enough to sacrifice their futures for this place. Iris could be studying, Anna could be enjoying her childhood, but instead they're here, watching their father give up."

"You don't understand-" Mr. Green's voice wavered.

"I understand plenty." James leaned forward. "I understand that life's been cruel to you. I understand that the farm is not as it used to be. But wallowing in it is a choice. And every day you make that choice, you're failing them all over again."

Iris's father seemed to deflate, his shoulders sagging. "I don't know how to fix it anymore... Everything I try seems to make things worse."

"Then try something different," James's expression softened slightly "If not for yourself, then for them. They deserve a father who fights back."

Mr. Green buried his face in his hands, his shoulders shaking. James stood up slowly.

"I apologize for speaking out of turn, sir. If you want me to pack my things and leave, I understand. But everything I said stands." He straightened his shoulders. "These women deserve better than this, and you're the only one who can give it to them."

* * *

Iris climbed the creaking stairs, her legs heavy with exhaustion. She paused outside Anna's door, hearing muffled sniffles from within. She knocked softly.

"Go away."

"It's just me." Iris pushed the door open to find Anna curled up on her bed, face buried in her pillow. She crossed the room and perched on the edge of the mattress. "Come here."

Anna threw herself into Iris's arms, her thin shoulders shaking. "Why is Father being like this again?"

Iris stroked her sister's tangled curls, working out the knots with gentle fingers. "He's scared, love. The farm isn't doing well, and he doesn't know how to fix it."

"But drinking won't help!" Anna pulled back, wiping her nose on her sleeve. "It only makes him mean."

"I know." Iris reached for the handkerchief in her

pocket and handed it to Anna. "Here, use this instead of your sleeve."

Anna blew her nose. "Remember when he used to read to us every night? Before..."

"Before Mother died." Iris smoothed Anna's hair back from her forehead. "He's still in there, you know. That father who read stories and taught us about the stars."

"How do you know?" Anna twisted the handkerchief between her fingers.

"Because I saw his face when you got top marks in arithmetic last time. He was so proud he couldn't stop smiling." Iris stood and crossed to Anna's desk, picking up the worn schoolbook lying there. "And I think it's time we helped him remember who he is."

Anna sat up straighter. "What do you mean?"

"I mean," Iris sat back down, opening the book to a dog-eared page, "that you're brilliant at your studies. You shouldn't have to miss school anymore to help at home."

"But we need…"

"We need you to be twelve." Iris tapped the arithmetic problems on the page. "To learn and grow and have adventures. That's what Mother would have wanted."

Anna's eyes widened. "What about you? Will you take the secretarial courses?"

Iris hesitated, then squared her shoulders. "Yes. I think I will. We can't put our lives on hold forever, waiting for things to get better."

"But the farm…"

"Will still be here." Iris stood and pulled Anna to her feet. "Come on, help me make a list."

She grabbed a pencil and paper from Anna's desk. Together they sat cross-legged on the floor, heads bent over the blank page.

"First," Iris wrote in neat letters, "Anna returns to school full-time."

Anna grabbed the pencil. "Second, Iris learns typing and takes the secretarial courses!"

"Third," Iris took the pencil back, "we help Father remember who he is."

"How?"

"By showing him we haven't given up." Iris drew a star next to each item. "He needs to see us fighting for our dreams. Maybe then he'll remember his own."

Anna leaned against her shoulder. "Do you really think we can do it?"

"I do." Iris wrapped an arm around her sister. "We're Greens. We're stronger than we think."

"Like Mother always said." Anna traced the words on their list. "I miss her."

"Me too." Iris squeezed her sister closer. "But she'd be proud of us, wouldn't she?"

Anna nodded against her shoulder. "Can I start tomorrow? With school?"

"We'll talk to Father in the morning." Iris folded the list carefully. "When he's... feeling better."

"What if he says no?"

"Then we'll keep trying until he says yes." Iris tucked the paper into her pocket. "Sometimes people need time to remember who they are. But we'll help him find his way back."

Anna yawned, exhaustion finally catching up with her. "Will you stay? Just for a little while?"

"Of course." Iris helped Anna into bed, tucking the blankets around her like their mother used to do. "Want me to tell you a story?"

"The one about the brave princess who saved her kingdom?"

Iris smiled. "Once upon a time, there was a princess who didn't need anyone to rescue her..."

CHAPTER 8

CHAPTER 8

James entered the barn at first light, his boots crunching on the scattered hay. Mr. Green stood by the workbench, organizing tools with mechanical precision.

"Mr. Green, about last night..." James cleared his throat. "I spoke out of turn. If you want me to pack my things—"

"Stop right there." Mr. Green set down a wrench with a sharp clank. "You said what needed saying. God knows I've been hearing it from Iris for years, but sometimes a man needs another man to tell him he's being a fool."

"Still, it wasn't my place."

"It became your place the moment you started caring about this farm and my girls." Mr. Green turned to face him, his weathered face etched with exhaustion. "My Annie, their mother, she'd have done worse than call me a coward. She'd have thrown me out of the house entirely."

James leaned against a support beam. "What was she like?"

"Strong. Clever. She saw straight through any nonsense I tried to pull." A ghost of a smile crossed Mr. Green's face. "The girls are just like her. Especially Iris."

"I can see that."

"The drinking..." Mr. Green's fingers drummed against the workbench. "It started after Annie passed. I thought it would help me sleep. Then I thought it would help me forget. Instead, I forgot who I was supposed to be for my daughters."

"It's not too late to remember."

"No, I suppose it's not." Mr. Green picked up a ledger from the workbench. "You mentioned having ideas about improving the farm. I'm ready to listen now, properly listen."

James straightened. "Are you sure?"

"Show me what you've got in mind."

"Well, first, we could diversify. The pigs are good, but we're vulnerable with just one source of income." James grabbed a piece of chalk and began sketching on the barn wall. "If we section off the north field, we could start with root vegetables. They're hardy, low maintenance."

"That field's been fallow for two years."

"Exactly. The soil's had time to recover. We could plant turnips first, then rotate with potatoes next season. And here—" James drew another section. "This area would be perfect for chicken coops. Fresh eggs fetch a good price at market."

Mr. Green studied the chalk marks. "The initial cost..."

"We can start small. Build one coop at a time, maybe six hens to begin with. Use salvaged wood from the old shed." James tapped the chalk against the wall. "The important thing is to have multiple streams of income. When one struggles, the others can carry us through."

"Like standing on three legs instead of one," Mr. Green mused.

"Exactly. And about the pigs, instead of trying to sell at market, we could approach the butcher shops directly. Let them see the quality for themselves."

"So basically, to cut out the middleman." Mr.

Green nodded slowly. "Annie used to say something similar. She said too many hands in the pot meant less soup for everyone."

"She was a smart woman."

"She was." Mr. Green's voice softened. "What else?"

James continued sketching. "The western pasture has good drainage. Perfect for an herb garden. Rosemary, thyme, sage amongst others are always in demand, and they take up little space."

"Iris would like that. She used to help her mother with the kitchen garden."

"We could start there then. Let her take charge of that project while she's doing her secretarial studies."

Mr. Green's head snapped up. "She told you about that?"

"Yes, sir. And I think it's a fine idea. The farm needs to adapt, and so do we all."

A long moment passed as Mr. Green studied the chalk drawings. "You really think we can turn things around?"

"I know we can. But it'll take all of us working together... What do you say? Shall we give it a proper go?"

Mr. Green clasped his hand firmly. "We shall. And James? Thank you."

James heard soft footsteps behind him as he wiped the chalk dust from his hands. Iris stood in the barn doorway, her long hair braided in two cornrows.

"Good morning," she said, stepping inside.

"Morning." He brushed his palms against his trousers. "Your father just left. I was just showing your father some ideas for the farm."

"I heard." She moved closer to examine the drawings. "I saw him walking back to the house. He looked... different. Lighter somehow."

"Listen, about last night—"

"Don't apologize." Iris shook her head. "You said what needed to be said. What I've been trying to tell him for months."

"Are you angry with me for interfering?"

"Angry?" She let out a small laugh. "No. If anything, I'm grateful. He actually listened to you."

James leaned against the workbench. "He's agreed to try some new approaches."

"He has?" Iris' eyes widened. "When I suggested changes last harvest, he wouldn't even consider it."

"What matters is that he's ready now. We can start small and build up gradually."

"What exactly did he agree to?"

"Root vegetables in the north field, chicken coops

near the old shed, and an herb garden in the western pasture." James tapped each section on the wall. "Plus, a new approach to selling the pigs, and crossbreeding"

Iris traced the chalk lines with her finger. "And you think this will work?"

"I know it will. But I'll need your help." He turned to face her. "Would you come with me to market tomorrow? We need to check the new feed prices, and I want to talk to some butchers about the Yorkshire pigs."

"The market?" She hesitated. "After what happened with Barnaby..."

"We're not going to sell, just gather information. Besides," he added with a slight smile, "I could use your sharp mind to help negotiate prices."

"Very well." Iris straightened her shoulders. "What time do we leave?"

"First light? We'll want to catch the butchers before they get too busy."

"I'll be ready."

James pushed away from the workbench. "I should get back to the pigs. I need to clean the troughs."

"I'll help." Iris reached for a nearby bucket.

"You're supposed to be taking it easy."

"Cleaning troughs isn't strenuous. Besides, I've been cooped up in that house for days." She lifted the bucket. "See? Perfectly capable."

James crossed his arms. "And what would Anna say?"

"Anna isn't here." Iris marched toward the pig pen. "Are you coming or not?"

He caught up to her in three strides. "At least let me carry that."

"I'm not an invalid, Mr. Brown."

"Back to Mr. Brown, are we?" He grinned. "And here I thought we'd made progress."

Iris set the bucket down by the first trough. "Fine. James. Though I'm beginning to regret allowing the familiarity."

"No, you're not."

She splashed some water in his direction. "Don't be so sure."

James dodged, laughing. "Careful now. I have excellent aim with a water bucket."

"Is that a threat?"

"Consider it a friendly warning." He grabbed the scrub brush. "I once won the village fair's water-carrying contest three years running."

Iris raised an eyebrow. "Impressive. Though I doubt your competition was particularly fierce."

"You'd be surprised. Mrs. Hodgkins was quite the contender."

"The baker's wife?" Iris snorted, then quickly covered her mouth.

"Don't laugh. She had excellent balance. She could carry three buckets at once."

"Now I know you're telling tales."

James dipped the brush in the water. "I never tell tales. Unlike some people who claim they can clean troughs faster than me."

"I never claimed that." Iris grabbed another brush. "Though I probably could."

"Care to make it interesting?"

Her eyes sparkled. "What did you have in mind?"

"First one to finish their side of the pen wins. Loser has to..." He pretended to think. "Help Anna with the washing up tonight."

"That's hardly fair. I already help with the washing up."

"Afraid you'll lose?"

Iris rolled up her sleeves. "Start counting."

James grinned. "One... two..."

She was already scrubbing before he said "three,". James matched her pace, stealing glances as she worked. A strand of hair had escaped her braid, curling against her neck. She'd pushed up her sleeves, revealing strong forearms tanned by the sun.

"Eyes on your own trough, Mr. Brown."

"Just making sure you're not cheating."

"I never cheat." She straightened, wiping her forehead with her sleeve. "I don't need to."

"No?" He increased his pace. "Because from where I'm standing, I'm at least two troughs ahead."

"Quality over speed."

"Excuses, excuses."

Iris flicked water at him again, this time catching his shirt. James retaliated, sending a spray of droplets in her direction. She squealed, a sound so unexpected and delightful it made him pause.

"That was underhanded," she accused, trying to suppress a smile.

"All's fair from where I stand."

"Is that how they do things at Thornfield Farm?"

"Oh no. We were much more civilized there." He adopted a pompous tone. "Water fights were strictly regulated affairs. Proper form was essential."

Iris laughed "You're ridiculous."

"You're enjoying it."

Their eyes met, and something shifted in the air

between them. Iris looked away first, her cheeks flushed. "We should finish these troughs."

"Right." James cleared his throat. "Though I believe I've already won."

"In your dreams, Mr. Brown." She attacked the next trough with renewed vigor. "In your dreams."

CHAPTER 9

CHAPTER 9

"Anna, watch your fingers!" Iris's voice cut through the early morning quiet like a knife, startling her younger sister into paying closer attention to the bread she was slicing. The last thing they needed was another reason to visit the doctor. Iris herself had only just clawed her way back from the brink, and she wasn't about to let anything set them back.

Anna shot Iris a sheepish grin. "Sorry! I was just thinking about school next week. It's hard to focus on bread when my mind's already in class."

Iris shook her head with a mixture of fondness

and exasperation. "Well, try to keep your mind and your fingers in the same place, please. The last thing we need is you missing school because of an accident in the kitchen."

"Will you buy those books for me at the market tomorrow?"

"I will," Iris confirmed, stirring the pot of porridge on the stove. She missed the warmth of the kitchen and the rhythmic motions of cooking. "James said he'd help me find a good bookseller. He's got an eye for quality, apparently."

Anna's eyes twinkled. "James this, James that. You seem to talk about him quite a lot."

Iris felt heat rise to her cheeks but kept her focus on stirring. "He works here now. It's only natural we talk about him."

Anna let out a theatrical sigh. "You know that's not what I meant."

"I have no idea what you're talking about," Iris replied with a level of indignation that didn't quite reach her eyes.

"Oh, come on," Anna teased, slicing another piece of bread with exaggerated care. "It's so obvious you like him."

Iris almost dropped the wooden spoon into the pot. "Anna! That's ridiculous."

"Is it?" Anna raised an eyebrow in that infuriatingly knowing way only a younger sister could manage. "Because I think you like him a lot more than you're willing to admit."

Iris glared at Anna, but there was no real malice in it. She couldn't stay mad at her sister for long, especially not when she had that earnest look on her face. "Fine," Iris huffed after a moment's pause, setting the spoon down with more force than necessary. "Maybe I do like him, but that doesn't mean anything can come of it."

Anna looked genuinely puzzled now. "Why not? He's kind, he's good-looking…"

"That's enough," Iris interrupted, holding up a hand as if to physically ward off further embarrassment.

Anna ignored her and pressed on. "He's great with the pigs and he's helping us turn this farm around. What's stopping you?"

Iris stammered, searching for words that wouldn't come out sounding like excuses even to her own ears. "Because… because it just can't happen."

"That's not a reason," Anna said firmly, crossing her arms over her chest.

"Alright then," Iris sighed heavily and turned to

face Anna directly. "Maybe I'm just not sure if I'm good enough for him."

Anna blinked in surprise before bursting into laughter.

"What's so funny?" Iris demanded, half annoyed and half curious.

"You," Anna said between giggles, wiping at her eyes as if she'd been laughing too hard for too long. "You think you're not good enough? Iris Green! You're smart, you're strong, you're beautiful, and any man would be lucky to have you."

Iris felt herself blushing again but didn't try to hide it this time. Instead, she let herself smile just a little bit at Anna's words.

"You really think so?" she asked quietly.

"I know so," Anna declared with conviction. "I've seen how James looks at you when he thinks no one's watching. I think he thinks so to."

"Anna—"

Iris heard the familiar creak of the front door and turned to see Mrs. Lucy stepping into the kitchen, a basket in one hand and a stack of books in the other. Mrs. Lucy was a stout woman with kind eyes that crinkled at the corners when she smiled, which she did often.

"Good morning, my dears!" Mrs. Lucy greeted

them warmly, setting the basket down on the table. "I brought some treats and a few new books for you, Iris."

Iris felt a wave of gratitude wash over her. Mrs. Lucy had always been like a second mother to her and Anna since their own mother had passed away. "Thank you so much, Mrs. Lucy," Iris said, moving to take the books from her. "You didn't have to go to all this trouble."

"Nonsense," Mrs. Lucy waved her off, her smile unwavering. "It's no trouble at all. I know how much you love to read."

Anna bounded over and plopped herself onto Mrs. Lucy's lap, making herself comfortable as if she were still a little girl instead of nearly a teenager. "What did you bring us today?" she asked eagerly.

"Let's see," Mrs. Lucy said, pulling out a small packet of biscuits from the basket and handing it to Anna before turning her attention back to Iris. "I also wanted to talk to you about your secretarial course."

Iris felt her cheeks warm slightly as she nodded. "I've been thinking about it a lot lately," she admitted. "I plan to register for the next session."

Mrs. Lucy beamed at her, pride evident in her

eyes. "That's wonderful news! I know you'll do great things with that education, Iris."

Anna chimed in, her mouth full of biscuit crumbs. "And I'm starting school again too!"

Mrs. Lucy's smile widened even further as she looked between the two sisters. "Your mother would be so proud of both of you," she said softly.

There was a brief silence as they all absorbed those words.

Mrs. Lucy broke the silence first, asking gently, "How is your father doing? And how's the farm coming along?"

Iris exchanged a quick glance with Anna before answering, "He's... trying his best," she said diplomatically. "We've had some setbacks, but we're working through them."

"And how about your new farmhand?" Mrs. Lucy asked with an interested tilt of her head.

Before Iris could respond, Anna piped up again with an impish grin on her face. "Oh, Iris likes him very much—"

"Anna!" Iris cut in sharply, feeling her face flush crimson as she chased Anna around the table amidst peals of laughter from her younger sister.

Mrs. Lucy watched them with amusement dancing in her eyes but didn't intervene until they had both collapsed into chairs once more, breathless but smiling.

"I see there's never a dull moment here," she remarked dryly.

"That's putting it lightly," Iris muttered under her breath while shooting Anna a look that promised retribution later.

Iris couldn't help but feel a flicker of embarrassment as Mrs. Lucy's amused eyes stayed on her. She glanced over at Anna, who was now busily devouring another biscuit, oblivious to the fact that she had just turned Iris's face the color of a ripe tomato. It wasn't like Iris to get flustered so easily, but then again, not much about life on the farm lately had been 'usual.'

"Well," Mrs. Lucy said with a knowing smile, "I'm sure James has been a great help around here."

Iris cleared her throat and nodded, trying to regain some semblance of composure. "He already has been. He's full of new ideas for the farm, and he's very... capable."

Mrs. Lucy tilted her head slightly, the crinkle around her eyes deepening as she studied Iris with a knowing gaze. "So, has James said anything to you about how he feels?" she asked casually, though Iris could sense the underlying curiosity in her tone.

Iris shifted uncomfortably glancing down at her hands as she fiddled with the edge of her apron. "No, he hasn't," she admitted softly. "It's just a useless crush. Nothing more."

Mrs. Lucy raised an eyebrow, her lips curving into a gentle smile. "Are you sure about that, dear? Sometimes these things have a way of sneaking up on you when you least expect them."

Iris felt a pang of frustration mingled with embarrassment as she met Mrs. Lucy's eyes. She appreciated the older woman's concern and wisdom, but this was starting to feel like an interrogation. "Really, Mrs. Lucy, it's nothing serious," she insisted, trying to sound more confident than she felt.

Anna chose that moment to chime in, still munching on her biscuit. "But Iris, you always talk about him and—"

"Anna," Iris cut her off with a stern look. "That's enough."

Mrs. Lucy chuckled softly and patted Anna's shoulder before turning back to Iris. "I understand, dear. But just remember that sometimes the best things in life come from the most unexpected places." She paused for a moment before adding thoughtfully, "You know, when I first met my

Matthew, I thought he was the most insufferable man I'd ever encountered."

Iris couldn't help but smile at that, despite herself. "Really?"

"Oh yes," Mrs. Lucy nodded emphatically. "He was stubborn and opinionated and drove me absolutely mad at times. But he also had a way of making me feel like I was the only person in the world who mattered to him." Her eyes grew distant for a moment as if she were reliving those memories.

Anna leaned forward eagerly, clearly enjoying the story. "And then what happened?"

Mrs. Lucy's smile widened as she looked at Anna and then back at Iris. "We fell in love, of course," she said simply. "It wasn't always easy, but it was worth every moment."

Iris felt a warmth spread through her chest at Mrs. Lucy's words but quickly pushed it aside with a sigh of exasperation. "Not you too," she grumbled half-heartedly.

Mrs. Lucy laughed gently and reached across the table to squeeze Iris's hand reassuringly. "I'm not trying to pressure you into anything, dear," she said kindly. "I just want you to be open to possibilities."

Iris nodded slowly, appreciating Mrs. Lucy's

gentle approach even if it did make her feel a bit vulnerable.

"Now," Mrs. Lucy continued briskly after a moment's pause, clearly sensing that it was time to change the subject for now. "What are your plans for today?"

CHAPTER 10

CHAPTER 10

James guided the horse-drawn buggy along the rutted road toward London's butcher district, stealing glances at Iris beside him. The morning fog had lifted, but a chill lingered in the air. Seven of their best pigs shuffled in the back, their grunts punctuating the clip-clop of hooves.

"We will go to Mr. Whitaker's shop first," James said, adjusting the reins. "He's known for fair prices, and his clientele appreciate quality meat."

"You seem to know every butcher in London,"

Iris remarked, gripping her seat as they made their way through a particularly deep rut.

"I had to learn fast at Thornfield. Mr. Patterson was particular about getting the best deals."

They pulled up outside Whitaker's Finest Meats, the shop's brass fixtures gleaming despite the early hour. A stout man with impressive mutton chops emerged, wiping his hands on his apron.

"Young Brown! Heard you'd left Thornfield." Mr. Whitaker's called to them from down the street. "These yours?"

"No. I'm working with the Greens now. Miss Green, this is Mr. Whitaker."

Iris nodded politely. "Pleasure, sir."

Whitaker circled their cart, examining the pigs with an expert eye. "Fine specimens. Not Yorkshires, though?"

"That's actually something we wanted to discuss," James said. "We're looking to improve our stock."

"Ah!" Whitaker's eyes lit up. "I just had old Ferguson in yesterday, talking about selling his prize Yorkshires. But first..." He patted one of their pigs. "I'll take all. Fifteen pounds each."

James felt Iris stiffen beside him. It was a good price, better than they'd hoped.

"Done," Iris said quickly, before Whitaker could reconsider.

While Whitaker's boys handled the pigs, he gave them directions to Ferguson's farm. "Tell him Oliver sent you. He's got the finest Yorkshires this side of the Thames."

They visited two more shops, gathering information about Yorkshire breeding and market demands. At the third shop, Buchanan's Quality Meats, they struck gold.

"Ferguson's here now," the wiry Mr. Buchanan told them, jerking his thumb toward the back. "He brought in some beauties this morning."

In the yard behind the shop, they found a tall man examining a massive Yorkshire boar. James heard Iris's sharp intake of breath.

"Good Lord," she whispered. "It's enormous."

The Yorkshire was easily twice the size of their largest pig, with a distinctive dished face and upright ears. Its pink skin was clean and healthy-looking.

"Robert Ferguson," the man introduced himself, extending a calloused hand.

"The size difference is remarkable," Iris said, circling the pen. "How do you manage the feed costs?"

"They convert feed more efficiently," Ferguson

explained. "Reach market weight faster too. I've got a breeding pair I'm looking to sell, if you're interested."

James watched Iris do the mental calculations. They had one hundred and five pounds from their morning sales, which was already more than they'd expected.

"What's your price?" James asked.

"Twenty-eight for each. The young sow's already bred, due in about three months."

Iris met James's eyes, and he saw the same excitement he felt.

"Would you take twenty-five?" Iris negotiated,

Ferguson stroked his chin. "Tell you what, since Oliver sent you, you can take it for twenty-six, and I'll throw in detailed breeding records and care instructions."

James watched Iris straighten her shoulders. "We'll take them."

James helped Ferguson secure the massive Yorkshire boar into their cart. The wooden slats creaked under the animal's weight, and he made a mental note to reinforce the pen walls back at Green Farm.

"Feed's crucial with these beauties," Ferguson said, patting the boar's broad back. "They'll eat you out of house and home if you let them, but they're efficient when managed right."

"What's your preferred mix?" James asked, checking the rope securing the sow.

Ferguson leaned against the cart. "Two parts barley to one part wheat middling's. Add in some protein. Fish meal works well if you can get it. The secret's in the timing though. Small meals, four times a day."

"Four times?" Iris brow furrowed. "That's double what we do now."

"Aye, but you'll see the difference. These aren't your common farm pigs." Ferguson reached into his coat and pulled out a worn leather notebook. "Here's my feeding schedule and notes from the last three years. Breeding dates, litter sizes, everything."

James accepted the notebook, thumbing through pages of meticulous records. "This is incredible, Mr. Ferguson."

"Call me Robert. Now, about breeding..." Ferguson moved to the sow's side. "This girl's carrying her first litter. She should farrow in about twelve weeks. Keep her separate from the boar until then. He's young and eager. You can keep him with a different sow, and you could have another breed."

James studied the sow's condition. She was indeed showing signs of pregnancy, her sides already beginning to round.

"Temperature's important during farrowing," Ferguson continued. "More so than with your other breeds. They need extra warmth in winter. I line the pen with fresh straw daily the week before they're due."

"What about the piglets?" James asked, thinking of their recent experience with Bessie's litter.

"Ah, that's where you'll see the real difference." Ferguson's eyes lit up. "Yorkshires average ten to twelve per litter, and the mothers are excellent. But you'll want to watch for crushing because these sows are heavy."

"Also install rails around the inside of the farrowing pen, about eight inches up from the floor. Gives the piglets somewhere to escape if the mother lies down suddenly."

Ferguson detailed everything from optimal pen size to breeding cycles, stopping occasionally to demonstrate proper handling techniques. His enthusiasm for the breed was infectious, and James found himself sharing Ferguson's excitement about their potential.

"One last thing," Ferguson said as they prepared to leave. "These are show-quality animals. Treat them right, and you could be looking at prize money at the county fair come autumn."

Show prizes could mean extra income, something the Green Farm desperately needed.

The Yorkshires settled into the cart, their massive bulk making it sit noticeably lower than usual. Ferguson handed James a small package wrapped in brown paper.

"Use this special feed mix to get you started. Remember - four times daily, like clockwork. They'll let you know if you're late."

James guided the horses homeward, beside him, Iris practically vibrated with excitement, clutching Anna's schoolbook to her chest.

"With the profit from today, we can keep Anna in school for quite a while," she said, her eyes bright. "I've been putting aside what I can, but this changes everything."

James smiled, enjoying her enthusiasm. Some loose strands of her hair had escaped her braid. "What about your own plans? The secretarial course you mentioned?"

"Well, these Yorkshires will need proper attention to start. You'll need help with the new feeding schedule, the breeding program..." She straightened her shoulders. "Once we have everything running smoothly, perhaps we could hire additional help. Then I could look into the courses."

"That's actually a solid plan," James adjusted the reins as they turned onto the main road. "We'll need about three months to establish the routine, maybe four to see the first results with the pregnant sow."

"Exactly." Iris nodded, then turned to face him more fully. "You know so much about farming. Have you always worked with livestock?"

James kept his eyes on the road, but his mind drifted back. "Since I was nine, actually. Moved from farm to farm, wherever they needed hands. I started at the Davies' place, mucking out stalls. Then the Millers, the Coopers..." He shrugged. "Learned something different at each one."

"Nine is very young," Iris said softly.

"The orphanage couldn't keep us past that age. Had to make our own way." He said it matter-of-factly, the way he always did. "No siblings either, so it was just me."

"James, I'm so sorry."

He glanced at her, saw the sympathy in her eyes, and shook his head. "Don't be. It's just life, isn't it? It made me who I am and taught me to work hard, to learn fast." He managed a small smile. "Besides, I got to see more of England than most people ever do."

"Still," Iris persisted, "it must have been difficult."

"It was, at first," he admitted. "But you get used to

it. Make your own family wherever you land. Like Mrs. Davies always saved me extra portions at supper. And old Cooper taught me everything I know about pigs." He chuckled. "Though these Yorkshires might be a different story altogether."

The cart hit a bump, making them both grab for stability. The massive Yorkshire boar in the back gave an indignant grunt.

"Well," Iris said, once they'd settled, "I suppose we'll learn about them together."

As they approached Green Farm, James spotted an elegant black buggy parked near the house, its polished brass fittings gleaming in the afternoon sun. He recognized the Wood family crest on the side panel and felt Iris tense beside him.

William Wood emerged from the house, in a tailored suit like the last one. His eyes narrowed as he took in their proximity on the cart bench, and James noticed how his hands clenched into fists at his sides.

"Miss Green," Wood called out, "I must say, I find it highly inappropriate for you to be gallivanting around the countryside alone with... the help."

James felt rather than saw Iris's spine stiffen. She waited until he brought the cart to a complete stop before responding.

"I beg your pardon?" Her voice was deadly quiet.

Wood stepped forward, adjusting his pristine cravat. "As the man courting you, I feel I must express my concern about your reputation."

"Courting me?" Iris's laugh was sharp and incredulous. "Mr. Wood, what on earth gave you that impression?"

Wood's face reddened. "Why, my proposal the other day—"

"During which I made myself perfectly clear that I was not interested," Iris cut in, her voice firm. "I rejected your proposal, Mr. Wood. In what world does that constitute courtship?"

CHAPTER 11

CHAPTER 11

"You're making a grave mistake," William's face darkened like storm clouds gathering. "A woman in your position should be more... practical about these matters."

Iris clenched as she climbed down from the buggy, her boots hitting the ground with force.

"My position?" she repeated "And what position would that be, Mr. Wood?"

William stepped closer, his expensive coat reeking of cologne that made her nose wrinkle. "An unmarried woman, struggling to keep a failing farm afloat. I'm offering you security, respectability." His lips curved in what he probably thought was a charming smile. "I'm willing to overlook your... previous rejection and start fresh. I'm here to court you properly, Miss Green."

A laugh escaped her "Court me? After insulting my home, my family, and my choices?"

"You're not seeing the bigger picture." William's voice dropped lower, meant for her ears alone. "Your father's drinking is common knowledge. The farm's debts are mounting. I could make all that go away with a signature on a marriage contract."

Fury blazed through her veins. "The only thing I'm not seeing is why you think I'd ever consider marrying someone who treats marriage like a business transaction and uses threats as courtship."

"Don't be foolish," he snapped, reaching out to grab her arm. His fingers dug into her flesh through her sleeve. "You need me whether you want to admit it or not."

Before Iris could wrench herself free, James said "Take your hands off her."

The words were quiet but carried such menace that William's grip loosened involuntarily. James stepped forward, his usual easy-going demeanor replaced by something harder, more dangerous. "Now."

William released her arm but didn't back away. "This doesn't concern you, farmhand. This is between me and my future wife."

"Future wife?" Iris rubbed her arm where his fingers had left marks. "Your delusions are getting worse, Mr. Wood."

"I suggest you leave," James said, moving to stand slightly in front of Iris. "Before you do something you'll regret."

William's face contorted with rage. "Are you threatening me? Do you know who I am?"

"I know exactly who you are," James replied evenly. "A man who thinks he can buy whatever he wants, including people. But Miss Green isn't for sale."

"And what makes you think you have any say in this matter?" William sneered, looking James up and down with obvious disdain. "You're nothing but hired help."

"Actually, Mr. Wood, you're interrupting a private moment between me and my future husband."

The words left her mouth before she could second-guess them. The shock on William's face would have been comical if the situation weren't so serious. His mouth opened and closed like a fish out of water.

"Your... future husband?" William's voice cracked. "This... this farmhand?"

Iris felt James stiffen beside her, but to his credit, he didn't contradict her statement. She moved closer to him, and his arm naturally settled around her waist, as if they'd done this a hundred times before.

"It can't be true," William sputtered, his face turning an alarming shade of red. "You're lying."

James, recovering admirably from his initial surprise, tightened his hold on Iris's waist. "It's true, Mr. Wood. And you're causing quite a scene on private property."

Iris fought to keep her expression neutral as she felt James's hand against her side. The lie felt surprisingly comfortable on her tongue, especially with James playing along so seamlessly.

William's gaze darted between them, searching for any sign of deception. "This is preposterous. A woman of your standing, engaging yourself to a... a farmhand?"

"A man of integrity and hard work," Iris corrected, letting genuine anger color her voice.

"Someone who respects me and this farm, unlike others I could mention."

William's face darkened. He straightened his coat with jerky movements, trying to salvage what remained of his dignity. "You'll regret this, both of you. Mark my words - you'll pay for what you've done here today."

"Good day, Mr. Wood," James said firmly, the dismissal clear in his tone.

They watched as William stomped back to his horse, mounted with less than his usual grace, and rode away. Only when he disappeared around the bend did Iris realize she was still pressed against James's side, his arm warm around her waist.

As William's horse disappeared from view, Iris became acutely aware of James presence beside her, his arm still curved protectively around her waist. The warmth of his touch seemed to seep through her dress, making her heart flutter in a way that had nothing to do with their recent confrontation.

She cleared her throat and stepped away, immediately missing his hold on her. "I... thank you. For backing up my rather impulsive claim."

James ran a hand through his hair, a faint flush coloring his cheeks. "Of course. Though I have to admit, that was quite the creative solution."

"I'm sorry for putting you in that position." Iris smoothed her skirts, desperate for something to do with her hands. "It just... came out."

"No need to apologize." His eyes met hers. "Sometimes the best way to deal with men like Wood is to give them something they can't argue with."

An awkward silence settled between them, and Iris found herself studying the ground, counting the pebbles scattered near her feet.

"I should..." James gestured toward the wagon where the new Yorkshire pigs waited. "These fellows need settling in their new home."

"Yes, of course." Iris nodded too quickly. "And I should head inside. Anna will want to hear about the market." She paused, then added, "The actual market part, not the... other thing."

James's lips twitched in what might have been a smile. "Probably wise."

They stood for another moment, neither quite ready to move, until Iris finally took a decisive step backward. "Right then. I'll just..." She pointed vaguely toward the house.

"Right," James echoed, already turning toward the wagon. "I'll get these pigs sorted."

Iris hurried toward the house, her cheeks burning. She didn't dare look back, though she could hear

James's boots on the gravel and the soft grunting of the pigs. Her heart was racing as if she'd run all the way from the market, and her waist still tingled where his arm had been.

She reached the kitchen door and slipped inside, pressing her back against it once it closed. What had she done? Claiming James as her future husband might have solved one problem, but it had certainly created another. How would they explain this to her father? To Anna? To anyone else who might have heard William's inevitable gossip?

But those were problems for later. Right now, she needed to collect herself before facing her sister's inevitable questions about their successful market trip. Questions that would have nothing to do with the way James's arm had felt around her waist, or how naturally he'd played along with her impulsive lie.

* * *

IRIS WAITED until after dinner to check on the new pigs. The evening air had cooled considerably, and she pulled her shawl tighter around her shoulders as she made her way to the pens.

She found James exactly where she expected him

to be, leaning against the fence of the new pen. His shirtsleeves were rolled up despite the chill, and his hair was slightly mussed as if he'd been running his hands through it.

"We really must stop meeting like this," Iris said, attempting to keep her voice light despite the memory of their earlier encounter with William Wood.

James turned, a slow smile spreading across his face. "At least this time there's no angry suitor in sight."

"Don't jinx it," she replied, grateful for the growing darkness that hid her blush. "William Wood might pop out from behind a hay bale."

"In that case, I'd better keep up appearances as your devoted future husband." His eyes sparkled with mischief in the fading light.

Iris's heart skipped, but she managed a laugh. "I'm never going to live that down, am I?"

"Not likely." He placed a finger to his lips, then beckoned her closer. "Come here."

She moved toward him, careful to keep her steps soft on the packed earth. When she reached his side, he pointed into the pen.

The new sow lay in a bed of fresh straw, her substantial bulk rising and falling with peaceful breaths. She looked completely at home, as if she'd always belonged at Green Farm.

"I thought they'd have trouble settling in," Iris whispered, surprised by how content the animal appeared.

James chuckled softly. "The boar's been pacing his pen like a caged lion, but this lady?" He gestured to the sleeping sow. "I think she's quite pleased to have a break from his constant attention."

Iris couldn't help but laugh at that, though she quickly muffled the sound with her hand. "Poor thing probably hasn't had a moment's peace for weeks."

"Can't say I blame her for enjoying the solitude," James agreed, his shoulder brushing against hers as he shifted his weight.

The evening air nipped at Iris's skin as she stepped away from the pig pen.

"Well, I should head back," she said, adjusting her shawl. "Anna will wonder where I've disappeared to."

"Iris, wait." James's voice stopped her mid-turn. "There's something I've been meaning to talk to you about."

Her stomach dropped. "You're not planning to resign, are you?" After everything that had happened today, the thought of him leaving made her chest tight.

"Far from it." He ran a hand through his hair, making it stand up even more. "Actually, I..." He cleared his throat, shifting his weight from one foot to the other. "About what happened earlier..."

"Oh, that." Iris felt her cheeks warm. "I'm sorry if I put you in an awkward position. I was just saying whatever came to mind to get rid of Wood."

"It wasn't 'whatever' to me."

The intensity in his voice made her breath catch. James stepped closer, close enough that she could see the nervous flutter of his pulse at his throat.

"When you said that, about me being your future husband..." He swallowed hard. "I know you were trying to get rid of Wood, but seeing him there today, thinking he had any claim to you... it made me realize I can't waste any more time. I like you, Iris. More than I probably should, given I work for your father."

Iris stood frozen, her heart hammering against her ribs as James continued.

"I know the timing might not be ideal, with everything happening on the farm, but..." He took a deep breath. "I'd like to court you. Properly."

When Iris didn't immediately respond, James

quickly added, "You don't have to answer now. Or ever, if you don't want to. I can take rejection if that's what you decide. I just... needed you to know."

Iris stared at him, taking in his expression, the way his hands were clenched at his sides as if to keep from reaching for her. The memory of his arm around her waist earlier flashed through her mind, how right it had felt.

"Yes," she said softly.

"Yes?" James's eyes widened slightly.

"Yes, you can court me."

CHAPTER 12

CHAPTER 12

"I think she's pregnant." James crouched beside the Yorkshire sow, his hands gentle on her flank.

Iris knelt next to him, her braid swinging forward as she leaned in to examine the pig. "Already? It's only been two weeks since we put her with the boar."

Two weeks. The same amount of time since that evening when William Wood's unwelcome visit had led to his real conversation about his feelings, and James still couldn't quite believe his luck. Every morning since then had felt brighter.

"The signs are there." He guided Iris's hand to the sow's belly. "Do you feel that? There's a slight swelling, and notice how she's been more docile lately?"

Their fingers brushed as they both explored the subtle changes in the animal's body. James felt that familiar spark of electricity at the contact. Iris didn't pull away, instead she let her hand rest under his as they monitored the sow's breathing.

"She does seem calmer," Iris admitted. "Usually, she's the first to make a fuss at feeding time."

James nodded, trying to focus on the task at hand rather than how close Iris was sitting. "Pregnancy will do that."

The sow grunted contentedly as they continued their examination. James shifted his position, his shoulder now touching Iris.

"Looks like our Yorkshire boy did his job. We should have piglets in about a month."

"Pure Yorkshire crosses," Iris said excitedly. "Mr. Ferguson will be pleased to hear his boar is proving his worth."

"Well," she said, her voice a touch breathier than usual, "I suppose this means our breeding program is off to a good start."

James couldn't help his grin. "Seems like quite a few things around here are off to a good start."

The blush deepened on Iris's cheeks, but she met his eyes with a smile that made his heart stutter.

"We should check her feed," Iris said, "If she is in pig, we'll need to adjust her diet."

"Already ahead of you." James gestured to the separate feed mix he'd prepared. "Ferguson's notes were very specific about nutrition during pregnancy. I've added extra minerals and adjusted the ratios."

Iris studied the feed mixture with obvious approval. "You think of everything, don't you?"

"I try to." He reached out and squeezed her hand briefly. "Especially when it matters."

Loose strands of hair that had escaped her braid, flew across her face and James had to resist the urge to brush them back.

"Well, isn't this cozy?" The youngest of the green announced her presence. "Should I tell Father you're too busy making eyes at each other to come to breakfast?"

James turned to see Anna leaning against the barn door, her grin wide and knowing. Iris dropped his hand immediately, though he noticed she was fighting back a smile.

"We were checking on the sow," Iris said, straightening her skirts. "She might be pregnant."

"Oh, I see?" Anna's eyebrows waggled suggestively.

James couldn't help but laugh at Anna's cheek. "The pigs really are breeding, little miss. Though I suppose your sister and I being sweet on each other isn't exactly a secret anymore."

"James!" Iris swatted his arm, but she was laughing too.

"What? It's true." He caught her hand and gave it a quick squeeze. "She knows, so no point denying it to your sister of all people."

Anna bounced on her toes. "Well, come on then, lovebirds. The eggs are getting cold, and Father's already at the table."

They followed Anna back to the house, James deliberately walking close enough to Iris that their shoulders brushed occasionally. The kitchen was warm and bright, with Henry already seated at the head of the table, studying what looked like bank statements.

"There you are," Henry said, looking up as they entered. He folded the papers and set them aside. "Good timing. I wanted to discuss something with you, James."

James took his seat, noting how Henry seemed more clear-eyed and steadier than he had in weeks. "What's on your mind, sir?"

Henry waited until they'd all settled, and Anna had served the eggs before speaking. "I've been thinking about taking a loan for the chicken coops, root vegetables, and all of it." He took a deep breath. "I'm going to the bank today. I'd like you to come with me."

Iris's fork clattered against her plate. "Father, are you sure? Taking out a loan is risky."

"I'm sure..." He looked at James. "You've shown me there's a way forward, son. I'd value your input when I speak to the bank manager."

James sat straighter in his chair, touched by both the trust and the invitation. "I'd be honored to help, sir."

Henry nodded. "We'll leave after breakfast. The bank opens at nine."

James caught Iris's concerned look and gave her what he hoped was a reassuring smile. This was a big step for Henry, showing real commitment to turning things around. The worry in Iris's eyes softened slightly, and she gave him a small nod.

Anna, who had been uncharacteristically quiet,

spoke up. "Does this mean we might get those fancy chicken coops James was talking about?"

"If the bank agrees, yes," Henry said. "And a proper herb garden too"

* * *

JAMES PULLED GENTLY on the reins, bringing their cart to a stop outside the imposing stone facade of the London Merchant Bank. The morning fog still clung to the cobblestones, and the air held that peculiar city dampness that made him miss the clean scent of fresh hay and open fields.

"Edward?"

The familiar figure straightened from his position by the bank's entrance, a worn cap pulled low over his eyes. Edward's face split into a wide grin as he recognized them.

"Jimmy!" Edward bounded down the steps, his new uniform somehow making him look both more distinguished and more out of place. "What brings you to this den of numbers and nightmares?"

"Loan application," James replied, helping Henry down from the cart. "When did you start working here?"

"Six weeks ago." Edward patted his slightly too-large coat. "Mary's due very soon. Twins, if you can believe it. Needed the extra work." His eyes crinkled with pride. "The pay's decent, and I only have to pretend to be proper during business hours."

James turned to see William Wood's distinctive black buggy pulling up to the curb, its polished brass fixtures gleaming even in the weak morning light. His stomach tightened. Nothing good ever came from Wood's presence.

"We should head inside," James said quietly to Henry, who had also noticed Wood's arrival.

The bank's interior smelled of leather and furniture polish. As they approached the secretary's desk, the young woman looked up, her quill pausing mid-stroke.

"May I help you, gentlemen?"

"James Brown and Henry Green to see Mr. Billings," James said, trying to project more confidence than he felt. "We have an appointment."

She consulted a leather-bound diary. "Ah yes, nine o'clock. Please, take a seat. Mr. Billings will be with you shortly."

They settled into the wooden chairs along the wall. James watched Henry fidget with his coat buttons. The older man had been unusually quiet during their journey, and James suspected he was thinking about the last time he'd asked for a loan.

A clock chimed somewhere in the building, and James found himself counting the seconds.

"Mr. Green? Mr. Brown?" The secretary's voice cut through his thoughts. "Mr. Billings will see you now."

They followed her down a narrow hallway lined with portraits of stern-faced men. The secretary knocked on a heavy oak door, then ushered them inside.

Mr. Billings sat behind a massive desk, his round face partially obscured by stacks of ledgers and papers. He was younger than James had expected, perhaps forty, with carefully combed hair and wire-rimmed spectacles that kept sliding down his nose.

"Gentlemen, please, be seated." Billings gestured to the chairs before his desk without looking up from whatever document held his attention. "I understand you're seeking a loan?"

"Yes, sir." Henry sat his hands gripping the arms of his chair. "We've recently acquired some Yorkshire breeding stock and wish to expand our operation."

This finally drew Billing's full attention. He set

down his papers and studied them over the rim of his spectacles. "Yorkshire pigs? That's quite an investment already. From whom did you purchase them?"

"Robert Ferguson," James supplied. "He's one of the most respected breeders in the county."

"Indeed." Billings pulled a fresh sheet of paper toward him. "And what exactly would this loan be used for?"

Henry glanced at James before answering. "We need to modify our existing facilities to accommodate the larger breed. New feeding systems, improved pens, and proper farrowing stalls. The Yorkshires require more specialized care than our traditional stock."

"I see." Billings made a note. "And your current income? How many pigs do you typically bring to market?"

Henry detailed their recent sales figures. He'd helped Iris prepare these numbers. Her neat handwriting filled the margins of their ledger with calculations and projections.

"Your existing debts?" Billings asked, not looking up from his notes.

Henry's voice wavered slightly. "We still owe some on the previous loan, but we've never missed a payment."

"Hmm." Billings set down his pen and removed his spectacles, polishing them with a silk handkerchief. "Unfortunately, gentlemen, I cannot offer you a loan at this time."

James felt as if the air had been sucked from the room. "May I ask why? Our projections show-"

"Your projections are just that... projections." Billings replaced his spectacles. "The bank must consider current circumstances, not potential futures. We'll keep your application on file, of course. Perhaps in six months, if your situation improves..."

"Our situation is improving," Henry insisted, leaning forward. "The Yorkshire breeding program-"

"Is a significant risk," Billings cut in smoothly. "One the bank is not prepared to support at this time. Now, if you'll excuse me, I have other appointments."

James recognized the dismissal for what it was. He stood, placing a steady hand on Henry's shoulder. "Thank you for your time, Mr. Billings."

They walked out of the office in silence, their footsteps echoing hollowly against the marble floor. The secretary didn't look up as they passed, her quill scratching steadily against paper.

Outside, the fog had lifted, but the day felt colder

somehow. Edward hurried over as they descended the steps, concern etched on his face.

"No luck then?"

James shook his head, helping Henry up into their cart. The older man's shoulders were slumped.

Edward glanced around before stepping closer, lowering his voice. "Listen, I probably shouldn't tell you this, but I overheard Wood and his friend as they left. They saw your cart arriving and... well, Wood went straight to billings' office. He said something about making sure certain parties didn't receive any assistance from the bank."

James's hands tightened on the reins. Of course, Wood would do this as a petty revenge for Iris's rejection.

"Jimmy?" Edward's voice carried a note of worry. "What are you going to do?"

"We'll figure something out," he said finally. "We always do."

Edward squeezed his arm. "Course you will. And if you need anything..."

"I know where to find you." James managed a smile. "Though I hardly recognize you in that fancy uniform."

"Oi!" Edward straightened his coat with mock

indignation. "I'll have you know I'm the most distinguished doorman this bank has ever seen."

"The only doorman this bank has ever seen, more like," James replied, some of the heaviness lifting from his chest.

"Get on with you then," Edward grinned, stepping back.

CHAPTER 13

CHAPTER 13

Iris set the bowls down, trying to read their faces. They'd been oddly quiet since returning from the bank, busying themselves with farm work and speaking only when necessary. Even Anna seemed to sense the tension, her usual chatter subdued as she arranged the bread and butter.

"So," Iris said, settling into her own chair, "how did things go at the bank?"

Her father stirred his stew without eating.

"Not as well as we'd hoped," James finally said,

"Mr. Billings was... less than receptive to our proposal."

"They rejected the application?" Iris was surprised to find her voice steady, her hands calm as she broke off a piece of bread.

Her father's spoon clattered against his bowl. "Wouldn't even properly consider it. He had his mind made up before we walked in."

"I see." Iris studied James's face, sensing there was more to the story.

"Edward works there now," James continued, reaching for the bread. "As a doorman. He overheard something interesting after we left."

Iris raised an eyebrow. "Oh?"

"Seems William Wood paid Mr. Billings a visit just before our appointment." James's jaw tightened. "Made sure certain parties wouldn't receive any assistance from the bank."

"Wood?" Anna's eyes widened. "That horrible man who wanted to marry Iris?"

"Anna," their father warned.

Iris should have felt angry. Should have felt the familiar surge of panic that accompanied any threat to their farm's stability. Instead, she found herself oddly calm as she considered their situation.

"Well," she said, breaking another piece of bread, "I suppose we'll have to find another way."

James looked up from his bowl, surprise flickering across his face. "You're taking this better than I expected."

"Am I?" Iris felt her lips curve into a small smile. "I suppose I am."

"Iris?" Her father's voice carried a note of confusion.

"It's just..." She gestured around the kitchen, taking in the warm stove, the well-worn table, the family gathered around it. "A few months ago, this would have terrified me. But now?" She met James's eyes. "We have healthy Yorkshire sows about to farrow. Our regular stock is thriving under the new feeding program. And we have you."

Color crept up James's neck. "I've been thinking about that, actually. About the harvest fair coming up."

"The harvest fair? Why?" Anna leaned forward, nearly knocking over her water glass.

"Easy there," Iris steadied the glass. "What are you thinking, James?"

He set down his spoon, enthusiasm lighting his features in a way that made Iris's heart flutter. "We don't need the bank. What we need are investors who understand farming. People who can see the value in what we're building here."

"The harvest fair is coming up. Every serious farmer and breeder in the county will be there. If we can show them our stock, demonstrate our breeding program..."

"They might be interested in investing," Iris finished, catching his excitement. "Especially with the piglets due soon."

"More than that," James continued. "The Yorkshires will reach about 600 pounds at full growth. That's nearly twice the size of our current stock. With proper feeding, they'll grow faster too - ready for market in about 6 months instead of 8."

Her father set down his glass. "You really think people would invest?"

"I know they would." James's confidence was infectious. "The Yorkshires alone will turn heads with the feeding plan."

"And if the sows farrow before then..." Iris did the calculations in her head. "A healthy Yorkshire litter could be 8 to 12 piglets. With our improved feeding program, we could show potential investors how quickly they gain weight."

"We can have more farrows..." Iris did the calculations in her head. "Healthy Yorkshire piglets would be quite the demonstration."

"Exactly..."

Her father cleared his throat. "It won't be easy. Getting everything ready while managing regular harvest work..."

"No," Iris agreed, "but when has anything worth doing ever been easy?"

"Well then," her father said, reaching for the breadbasket, "I suppose we'd better start planning."

After dinner, Iris gathered the empty bowls while Anna rushed off to sleep so she can wake up early for school. Her father retreated to his study, leaving her alone with James in the quiet kitchen.

"I'll wash," James offered, rolling up his sleeves.

"I can manage-"

"I know you can." He smiled, already pumping water into the basin. "But I'd like to help."

Iris picked up a drying cloth, falling into step beside him as naturally as they did during their morning farm work. The gentle splash of water and clink of dishes filled the comfortable silence.

"I've been thinking," James said, handing her a cleaned bowl.

"A dangerous pastime."

"Very funny." He flicked water in her direction. "I

was thinking we haven't had much time alone since... well, since I asked to court you."

Iris focused intently on drying the bowl. "We see each other every day."

"Yes, while mucking out pig pens or discussing feed schedules." He passed her another dish. "Not quite what I had in mind for courting."

"What did you have in mind?"

"Would you like to go to town with me tomorrow? After the morning chores?"

Iris set down her cloth. "James, we shouldn't-"

"Be alone?" He laughed softly. "We'll be in the middle of town, surrounded by half the county.... come to town with me. We can look at books, have lunch at that little cafe by the bookshop. I promise to maintain a respectable distance at all times."

"All times?" She found herself smiling despite her attempts not to.

"Well, maybe not when helping you down from the cart. That would be terribly ungentlemanly."

"We do have a lot to prepare for the harvest fair..."

"Which is exactly why we should take one afternoon." James dried his hands on a spare cloth. "Clear our heads, make proper plans without Anna interrupting every five minutes."

Iris laughed "She means well."

"She does. But I'd like a few hours with just you." His voice softened. "No pigs, no farm accounts, no elaborate fair preparations. Just us."

"So?" he prompted. "Will you come to town with me tomorrow?"

"Yes." The word came out before she could second-guess herself. "But we should leave early, before the afternoon heat."

"I'll have the cart ready after morning feeding." His smile brightened the dimming kitchen.

"We could also look at some books for your secretarial course."

"I haven't even registered yet."

"But you will." His voice held such certainty that she had to look at him. "You should, Iris. You're brilliant with numbers and organization. The farm's books have never been clearer since you took them over."

"That's different. That's just–"

James raised an eyebrow. "Just keeping track of breeding schedules, feed costs, market prices. That sounds exactly like what a secretary does, only you're doing it while also running a farm."

Iris felt her cheeks warm. "You make it sound grander than it is."

"You make it sound smaller than it is." He handed her the last plate, his fingers lingering against hers.

"James—"

"I mean it." His voice was gentle but firm. "You've put everyone else first for so long. Let someone else do that for you, just a little."

Iris felt her throat tighten. "And what if I'm not good enough? What if I fail?"

"Then you'll try again." He shrugged as if it were the simplest thing in the world. "But you won't fail. You're the most capable person I know."

"After yourself, you mean?"

"Oh no," he grinned. "I still can't tell your mother's bread recipe from Anna's experimental versions. You're clearly the superior talent here."

"That's because you eat whatever's put in front of you like a starving farmhand."

"I am a starving farmhand. Growing all these prize-winning pigs works up an appetite."

They hadn't moved, but somehow the space between them felt smaller. Iris could see the laugh lines around his eyes, the small scar on his chin from some long-ago farm accident.

"We should finish these dishes," she said softly.

"We should." But he didn't move.

CHAPTER 14

CHAPTER 14

The morning sun hadn't quite burned through the fog when James brought the cart around. Iris stood on the porch, fidgeting with her shawl. She'd changed her dress three times before settling on her mother's old blue one, not that she'd admit to such frivolity. The fabric swished softly against her ankles as she stepped out into the morning.

"Good morning," James called softly. He'd attempted to tame his usually unruly hair. The sight made something flutter in her chest.

"You're early," she said, hoping her voice didn't betray how long she'd been waiting at the window.

"Couldn't sleep." He hopped down from the cart, and the way he looked at her made her cheeks warm. "You look beautiful."

"It's just an old dress."

"It's blue." He stepped closer, offering his hand. "Like the morning sky just before sunrise."

"When did you become a poet, Mr. Brown?" But she placed her hand in his, letting him help her into the cart.

"Must be all those verses Anna's been reading to the pigs." His fingers lingered against hers a moment longer than necessary. "They're rubbing off on me."

The cart shifted as he climbed up beside her, bringing them closer. Neither moved away.

"I half expected Anna to insist on chaperoning," James said as they set off.

"Oh, she tried." Iris adjusted her shawl, hiding a smile. "But Father reminded her that school takes precedence over spying on her sister."

"And what does your father think about... this?" He gestured between them with his free hand.

"He thinks you're a good man." Iris watched his profile as he guided the horses. "Though he did mention something about having a shotgun if you prove him wrong."

James's laugh rumbled "A shotgun? I should be terrified, but somehow it's reassuring. It shows he cares about you."

"He's been different lately," Iris said, watching the familiar countryside roll past. "More like his old self."

"And is that why you finally agreed to come to town with me? Because your father approves?"

"No… I agreed because... because being with you feels like breathing."

James's hands tightened on the reins. "Iris..."

"I mean," she rushed on, suddenly flustered by her own honesty, "you make everything feel easier. Natural. Like those mornings in the pig pen when we're working together and oh lord, I'm comparing our courtship to pig farming."

"Please don't stop," James said, and she could hear the smile in his voice. "I find pig farming quite romantic."

"You would." But she was smiling too, the earlier nervousness melting away. "Though I suppose it's fitting. We did have our first conversation over a feed trough."

"And our first argument about proper feeding schedules."

"That wasn't an argument. That was me being stubborn."

"Was?" He raised an eyebrow. "Past tense?"

Iris flicked his arm. "Don't push your luck, Mr. Brown."

They fell into silence as the cart rounded the bend toward town. The morning mist was finally burning off, revealing a sky as blue as Iris's dress. Market-day crowds were already gathering, the streets coming alive with vendors setting up their stalls.

"Where shall we start?" James asked as he helped her down from the cart, his hands warm at her waist. "The bookshop? Or perhaps that café you mentioned?"

"First," Iris said firmly, "you're going to buy me one of Mrs. Son's apple tarts while they're still warm from the oven."

"Am I now?"

"Yes. And then you're going to tell me how you got that scar on your chin, because I've been wondering for weeks."

James touched the small mark self-consciously. "It's not a very exciting story."

"I want to hear it anyway." She took his offered arm, hyper-aware of the solid warmth of him beside her. "I want to hear all your stories."

They made their way down the cobbled street, with Iris's hand tucked into James's arm. Mrs. Son's bakery sat on the corner, the scent of fresh bread and pastries wafting through its open door.

"Morning, dears!" Mrs. Son called as they entered, her round face flushed from the ovens. Her eyes sparkled at the sight of them together. "Don't you two make a handsome pair."

Iris felt her cheeks warm as James purchased the promised apple tarts. They were still warm, wrapped in paper that crinkled as they found a quiet spot near the town square fountain.

"Now then," Iris said, breaking off a piece of tart, "that scar?"

James touched his chin again, a bashful gesture she was beginning to find endlessly endearing. "You'll be disappointed. It wasn't from wrestling a bull or fighting off bandits."

"Tell me anyway."

"I was seven," he said, leaning back against the fountain's stone edge. "There was this cat at the orphanage. it was a mean old thing, but I was determined to make friends with it. One day I cornered it in the kitchen..."

"Oh no."

"Oh yes." He grinned. "Turns out cats don't appreciate being forcibly befriended. Who knew?"

Iris couldn't help but laugh. "So, you were stubborn even then?"

"Says the woman who refused to admit my feeding system was better for three whole weeks."

"Two weeks at most." She took another bite of tart, savoring the sweet apple and buttery pastry. A dot of filling clung to her bottom lip, and before she could reach for her handkerchief, James's thumb brushed it away.

Time seemed to stop. His touch lingered at the corner of her mouth, feather-light but sending sparks through her entire body. Their eyes met, and Iris forgot how to breathe.

James pulled back first, clearing his throat. "Sorry, I shouldn't have—"

"It's alright." Her voice came out unusually husky. "I don't mind."

Around them, the town went about its morning business, but in that moment, it felt like they were in their own world.

"Tell me something else," Iris said, desperate to

break the tension before she did something scandalous like kiss him in the middle of the square. "Something from before we met."

James shifted slightly, their shoulders brushing. "What would you like to know?"

"Everything." The word escaped before she could temper it. "I mean... tell me about your happiest memory."

His expression softened. "It might surprise you."

"Try me."

"It was at the Davies' farm. That was my first placement after the orphanage. Mrs. Davies caught me reading in the barn when I should have been working." He smiled at the memory. "Instead of scolding me, she sat down in the hay and asked me to read to her. Said her eyes weren't what they used to be."

"Was that true?" Iris asked, already suspecting the answer.

"Not even slightly. She had the sharpest eyes of anyone I knew. Could spot a loose fence post from fifty paces." He chuckled. "But every afternoon after that, while the bread was baking, she'd find me in the barn. We went through three books that summer."

Iris watched his face as he spoke, struck by how

the memory lit him up from within. "What did you read?"

"Adventure stories mostly. Tales of far-off places I'd never see." He met her eyes. "Though lately I'm finding adventure closer to home."

"In pig farming?" she teased, trying to lighten the moment before her heart burst.

"In unexpected meetings with stubborn women who challenge everything I think I know."

"James..." Her voice wavered.

"I know." He took her hand, his thumb tracing patterns on her palm. "Too much?"

"No," she whispered. "Not enough."

A group of ladies walked past, their curious glances making Iris suddenly aware of their public position. She started to pull away, but James kept hold of her hand.

"Let them look," he said quietly. "I'm not ashamed of how I feel about you."

"And how do you feel?" The question slipped out before she could stop it.

James turned to face her fully, his expression serious. "Like I've been wandering my whole life, taking any work that came my way, never staying in one place long enough to call it home. Then I saw you and suddenly..." He swallowed hard. "Suddenly I couldn't imagine being anywhere else."

Iris's heart thundered in her chest at his words. The honest vulnerability in his expression made her want to reach for him, propriety be damned. Instead, she squeezed his hand tighter.

"The first time I saw you," she said softly, "you were helping Father with those escaped pigs. I watched from the window, thinking how efficiently you moved, how naturally you seemed to understand what needed doing." She smiled at the memory. "Then you had to go and rearrange my whole feeding system."

"Which worked better," he couldn't help adding.

"Which worked better," she conceded, nudging his shoulder with hers. "Though I'll deny saying that if you tell anyone."

The morning had grown warmer, the square filling with more townspeople.

"We should probably walk," Iris said reluctantly. "Before the gossips have us married with six children by sundown."

James stood, helping her to her feet. "Only six? I'm disappointed in their lack of imagination."

They strolled through the market, arms linked, pausing occasionally to examine vendors' wares. At the flower stall, James bought her a small bouquet of wildflowers, their purple and yellow petals bright against her blue dress.

"These remind me of the ones that grow near the pig pen," he said, tucking one behind her ear.

"Of course they do." She touched the flower gently. "Everything comes back to pigs with you."

"Not everything." His voice dropped lower, meant just for her. "Sometimes I think about the way you look in the morning light, or how your eyes crinkle when you're trying not to laugh at one of my terrible jokes."

"They are terrible," she agreed, but her smile gave her away.

They completed their circuit of the market, neither quite ready to head home yet. The day stretched before them, full of possibility.

"One more stop," James said, guiding her toward a small café tucked between the tailor's shop and the post office. "I hear they make excellent tea."

Inside, they found a quiet corner table. James pulled out her chair, and Iris was struck by how natural it felt, sitting here with him like this. As if they'd been doing it for years instead of hours.

The afternoon passed in a blur of shared tea and stories. James told her about his years moving from farm to farm, and Iris shared memories of her mother, things she hadn't spoken of in years.

When they finally headed home, the sun was low in the sky, painting everything in soft golden light. The cart swayed gently as they traveled the familiar road back to the farm.

James drew the horses to a stop, turning to face her fully. "Iris, you've always been more. I just hope someday you'll see yourself the way I see you."

In the fading light, with the countryside spread out around them and no prying eyes in sight, Iris gathered her courage. She leaned forward and pressed a soft kiss to his cheek.

"How's that for scandalous?" she whispered.

James's smile could have lit up the darkening sky. "Worth every bit of gossip tomorrow."

They arrived home just as the first stars appeared. Anna was waiting on the porch, practically bouncing with curiosity, but Iris found she didn't mind. She had a pocket full of wildflowers, the memory of James's smile, and the feeling that something fundamental had shifted in her world.

She'd always thought love would feel like drowning, like being swept away. Instead, it felt like coming home.

CHAPTER 15

"If you polish that pig any more, she'll blind the judges," Iris teased, appearing at James's elbow as he worked another coat of oil into the Yorkshire sow's hide.

Dawn had barely broken over the fairgrounds, but they'd been up for hours preparing. The morning air held that particular autumn crispness that promised a perfect day for the harvest fair.

"She needs to look her best." James ran the cloth over the sow's broad flank again. "These aren't just any judges we need to impress. Ferguson himself will be here."

"Ferguson?" Iris's eyes widened. "You didn't tell me that."

"I wanted it to be a surprise." He grinned at her expression. "He's bringing potential investors with him. He said our breeding program caught his attention."

"No pressure then," Iris muttered

The Yorkshire sow grunted contentedly as James moved to check her ears. Six healthy piglets dozed in the straw beside her, their pink hides gleaming in the early light. This same sow was the first piglet from the Ferguson's pair.

"They're perfect," Iris said softly, reaching down to stroke one of the sleeping piglets. "Even Wood himself couldn't find fault with them."

"Speaking of Wood..." James straightened, wiping his hands on a cloth. "I heard he'll be here too. His father's one of the fair's patrons."

"Wonderful." Iris's voice dripped with sarcasm. "Perhaps he'd like to invest in his jilted almost-fiancée's pig farm."

"Well, technically," James caught her hand, pulling her closer, "he was jilted by my future wife, so I'd say that's his loss and my considerable gain."

The words slipped out before he could catch them. They hadn't discussed marriage, not really, though that hasty lie to Wood had somehow grown into something that felt remarkably like truth.

Before she could respond, Anna's called out across the fairgrounds.

"They're setting up the judging pavilion! And you'll never guess who's here already!" Anna came running, her boots kicking up dust. "Mr. Ferguson brought Lord Ashworth's brother with him. The one who's been buying up breeding stock all over the county!"

James felt Iris tense beside him. "Ashworth? The same family that…"

"Bought Patterson's farm, yes." James squeezed her hand. "But Thomas Ashworth is different from his brother. He actually knows farming, and he breeds horses up north."

"And how do you know that?" Iris raised an eyebrow.

"Because he's standing right behind you," a deep voice interrupted, amused. "Though I prefer Tom to Thomas."

They turned to find a tall man in riding clothes, his resemblance to Lord Ashworth clear but softened by laugh lines around his eyes. Ferguson stood beside him, beaming like a proud father.

"When Ferguson told me about your Yorkshire

breeding program, I had to see for myself." Tom's gaze swept over their pigs appraisingly. "Those are Ferguson's lines, but you've done something different with the feeding, haven't you?"

James blinked in surprise. "Yes, sir. We modified the traditional schedule to…"

"Four smaller meals instead of two large ones?" Tom nodded approvingly. "I tried that myself with horses. It's tricky to manage but worth the effort." He crouched to examine the piglets. "They have such remarkable coat quality. What are you using for supplements?"

"Fish meal and wheat middling's," Iris answered, her earlier tension melting into enthusiasm. "And we've added fresh herbs to their feed."

"Innovative." Tom straightened, brushing off his knees. "Ferguson tells me you're looking for investors."

"We are." James felt Iris's hand slip into his. "We have plans to expand the breeding program, perhaps add some dairy stock as well."

"Diversification. Smart." Tom exchanged looks with Ferguson. "I'd like to discuss terms after the judging…" He gestured to where a small crowd was gathering near the pavilion. "Shall we?"

"If you'll excuse us," Ferguson cut in, "the judges

need to examine the stock before the crowds arrive. Miss Green, might we borrow your young man?"

"Of course," Iris said, "Though I'm not sure anyone ever really borrows James - he tends to do exactly what he thinks is right regardless."

"I believe that's why we like him," Tom laughed. "Come on, Brown. Show me these feeding pens you've designed."

As James walked away with the two men, he caught snippets of Anna's excited chatter to Iris - something about dancing and fairy lights being strung up for the evening festivities. But his attention was quickly drawn to the task at hand as more judges gathered around their pens.

"Extraordinary muscle development," one judge commented, running practiced hands over their prized Yorkshire boar. "And you say this was achieved without excessive grain?"

"Yes, sir." James outlined their feeding program, watching Tom Ashworth nod approvingly at each detail. "The herbs seem to aid digestion, leading to better feed conversion."

"Revolutionary," another judge murmured. "Though some might call it unconventional."

"Some called crop rotation unconventional once,"

Tom interjected smoothly. "Now it's standard practice. Progress requires innovation, gentlemen."

The morning passed and James found himself repeatedly explaining their methods, each time and watching understanding dawn in the eyes of experienced farmers and breeders. By midday, a crowd had gathered around their pens, and he heard the distinct sound of betting on the judging results.

"Your father would be proud," Henry's voice came from behind him. James turned to find Iris's father watching the proceedings with bright eyes. "Though not nearly as proud as I am."

"Mr. Green—"

"Henry," he corrected. "Just Henry. I gave you permission before. Especially now that you court my daughter."

James felt heat rise to his cheeks. "Sir, I—"

"Just make sure you save her a dance tonight," Henry said with a knowing smile. "The harvest dance was where I first courted her mother, you know."

Before James could respond, a bell rang out across the fairgrounds, signaling the judges' deliberation. The crowd's excited murmur grew louder.

"Here we go," Tom appeared at James's elbow.

"Though I'd say the investors' interest is already worth more than any ribbon."

"First prize for breeding stock," the head judge announced, to the hushed crowd. "Green Farm, for their exceptional Yorkshire program."

The surge of pride in James's chest was overwhelming. Through the applauding crowd, he caught sight of Iris, her face glowing with triumph. Anna bounced beside her, practically vibrating with excitement.

"Well deserved," Tom clasped his shoulder. "Now, about that investment discussion…"

"Brown!" A sharp voice cut through the celebration. William Wood stood at the edge of the crowd, his father beside him. "I see you've managed to fool the judges with your… creative farming methods."

"The only fool here is one who can't recognize quality stock," Tom said mildly, stepping forward. "Wouldn't you agree, Richard?" He addressed the elder Wood directly.

"Thomas." Wood Senior's tone shifted noticeably. "I wasn't aware you were involved with this… enterprise."

"Quite involved, actually. I'm investing heavily in their breeding program." Tom's casual announcement sent a ripple through the watching crowd. "In fact, several of us are. Wouldn't want to miss out on such an opportunity."

James watched the Woods' faces shift from disdain to barely concealed interest. William's complexion had turned an interesting shade of purple.

"Now then," Tom turned back to James, deliberately dismissing the Woods. "Let's discuss numbers over lunch. I have some ideas about expanding those feeding pens of yours."

By the time the sun began to set, they had secured not only Tom's investment but commitments from three other prominent farmers.

As twilight descended, the fairgrounds transformed. Lanterns were strung between trees, their soft light creating pools of gold in the growing darkness. The sound of fiddles being tuned drifted across the evening air.

"There you are." Iris appeared beside him, changed into her blue dress, the one she'd worn on their first outing to town. "I was beginning to think the investors had stolen you away entirely."

"Never." James took in the sight of her, backlit by lantern light. "You look beautiful."

"You said that this morning."

"It was true then too." He offered his hand. "Dance with me?"

The musicians struck up a waltz. Other couples were already moving onto the makeshift dance floor, but James barely noticed them. Iris's hand was warm in his as he led her into the dance.

"We did it," she said softly as they turned. "The farm is safe."

"Was there ever any doubt?"

"Several hundred doubts, actually." Her eyes sparkled up at him. "But somehow you made me believe anyway."

CHAPTER 16

CHAPTER 16

James studied the farm accounts with satisfaction, the morning light streaming through the barn office window. Two months had passed since their triumph at the harvest fair, and the changes were already evident. Tom Ashworth's investment had allowed them to expand the Yorkshire breeding program faster than they'd dared hope. The new feeding pens gleamed with fresh wood, and the sound of content pigs drifted through the open window.

But it wasn't just the farm that was flourishing.

James couldn't help but smile as he heard Anna's voice floating across the yard, reciting her Latin conjugations as she headed for the cart that would take her to school. Her newfound confidence radiated in everything she did, from her improved marks to the way she carried herself.

"Amo, amas, amat," she called out cheerfully to the pigs as she passed. The Yorkshire sow raised her head at the sound, as if appreciating the impromptu Latin lesson.

"I don't think the pigs speak Latin yet," James called out, emerging from the office.

Anna spun around, her books clutched to her chest. "But they might! Mrs. Lucy says learning is never wasted." Her eyes sparkled with the kind of enthusiasm that only a thirteen-year-old discovering the world could muster. "Did you know in Ancient Rome they had special pig markets? We learned about them yesterday."

"Is that so?" James leaned against the doorframe, enjoying her excitement. "And did they have Yorkshire pigs in Ancient Rome?"

"Well, no," Anna admitted. "But they had something called a 'sus scrofa domesticus' which is Latin for—"

"Domestic pig," Iris's voice completed the

sentence as she rounded the corner of the barn. "Someone's been paying attention in her lessons."

James's heart did that familiar skip it always did at the sight of her. She wore her hair in a simple braid today, with a few wayward strands framing her face as usual. Even in her practical work dress, she managed to take his breath away.

"James has been checking the accounts again," Anna reported with the air of someone sharing important gossip. "He's been in there since dawn. I think he's planning something."

Iris raised an eyebrow in his direction. "Is that so?"

"Can't a man review his ledgers in peace?" James protested, though he couldn't quite meet her eyes.

"Not when it's my birthday," Iris pointed out. "And especially not when my nosy sister has been hinting at surprises all week."

Anna gasped in mock offense. "I haven't been hinting! I've been very subtle."

"As subtle as a Yorkshire boar in a china shop," James muttered, earning a giggle from Anna and an eye roll from Iris.

"The cart's waiting, little scholar," Iris reminded her sister. "You don't want to be late for your history lesson. I hear there might be more fascinating facts to learn."

Anna gathered her skirts and practically skipped toward the waiting cart. "Don't forget about tea with Mrs. Lucy later!" she called over her shoulder. "She says she has a special delivery!"

As Anna disappeared down the drive, Iris turned to James with suspicious eyes. "You wouldn't happen to know anything about this special delivery, would you?"

"Me?" James adopted his most innocent expression, the one that never fooled her. "I'm just a simple farmhand, remember?"

"A simple farmhand who's been conspiring with my sister and our friend." She stepped closer, and James caught the faint scent of lavender that always seemed to cling to her. "Should I be worried?"

"Never." He reached out and tucked one of those wayward strands behind her ear, his fingers lingering perhaps a moment longer than strictly proper. "Though you might want to wear your new blue dress for tea."

"James Brown, are you giving me fashion advice?"

"I would never presume." He grinned. "Though I do recall a certain blue dress at a certain harvest fair that made me forget my own name for a moment."

A blush crept up her neck, but her eyes held his steadily. "That was quite a day."

"It was." He wanted to pull her closer, to kiss her right there in the morning sun, but the sound of approaching footsteps reminded him of their surroundings. Henry their new farm hand appeared around the corner, his limp less pronounced these days thanks to the new tonic from Doctor Morrison.

"Morning, you two," Henry called out cheerfully. "Iris, cam you get me a cup of water."

"Father, you should be walking around," Iris sighed, "please sit, I'll be back soon."

As Iris headed toward the house, Henry turned to James with a knowing look. "Everything ready for this afternoon?"

James nodded, his hand instinctively touching his vest pocket where a small velvet box had resided for the past week. "Mrs. Lucy will bring the papers at tea, and then..."

"And then," Henry's eyes crinkled with warmth, "you'll make an honest woman of my daughter. Assuming she says yes."

"That's still not guaranteed," James reminded him, though his heart raced at the thought.

"Oh, I wouldn't worry too much about that." Henry clapped him on the shoulder.

"I hope I can make her as happy as she deserves."

"You already do, son." Henry's voice was gruff with emotion. "Now, let's check those new pig pens before I turn into a sentimental old fool."

James threw himself into farm work, trying to keep his mind off the afternoon ahead. He checked and rechecked the Yorkshire pens, monitored the pregnant sows, and even helped their new farm hand repair a loose board in the chicken coop, all while the small velvet box seemed to burn a hole in his pocket.

As the afternoon approached, James found himself growing increasingly nervous. He changed his shirt twice, much to the amusement of Henry, who caught him examining his reflection in the barn window.

"If you smooth down your hair one more time," Henry called out, "it might just give up and abandon you entirely."

"Very funny." James tugged at his collar. "I just want everything to be perfect."

"Perfect is overrated," Henry said wisely. "Annie once told me that the best moments in life are the imperfect ones. They're more memorable that way."

Before James could respond, they heard the distinct sound of Mrs. Lucy's cart approaching.

Anna's spoke with excitement as she ran out to greet their visitor.

"You're early!" Anna exclaimed. "Is everything ready? Did you bring the—"

"Anna," Mrs. Lucy's warm voice held a note of warning. "Let's not spoil any surprises, shall we?"

James took a deep breath and headed toward the house. Through the kitchen window, he could see Iris in her blue dress – she'd taken his advice after all – helping to set up for tea. His heart felt too big for his chest.

The kitchen was warm and bright when he entered, filled with the scent of fresh bread and something sweeter. Had Anna attempted another cake? Mrs. Lucy was already settled at the table, a mysterious package beside her chair. Henry took his usual seat while Anna practically vibrated with excitement as she arranged teacups.

Iris, beautiful in her blue dress, looked at him with that mixture of suspicion and affection that never failed to make his pulse race.

"Well," she said, hands on her hips, "are you going to tell me what all this mystery is about?"

James exchanged glances with Mrs. Lucy, who nodded encouragingly. "Actually," he said, reaching for the wrapped package Mrs. Lucy handed him, "I have something for you."

"James..." Iris started to protest, but he cut her off gently.

"Please. Let me do this properly."

He placed the package in her hands, watching as she carefully unwrapped it. The room held its breath as she revealed the course registration papers.

"I don't understand," Iris whispered, her fingers tracing the official letterhead. "This is..."

"Your future," James said softly. "If you want it."

"But how did you...?" She looked up at him, her eyes bright with unshed tears. "The course fees alone..."

"Are taken care of," Mrs. Lucy interjected gently. "Consider it a joint birthday gift from all of us who love you."

Iris seemed overwhelmed, looking around at all the faces watching her with such love and expectation. "I don't know what to say."

"Say you'll take it," James stepped closer, taking her hands in his. "Say you'll let yourself have this dream."

"But the farm..."

"Will still be here," Henry assured her. "James and I can manage, especially with Tom's investment. We have hired 2 hands, and we'll hire 2 more to make it easier as we grow. And you'll only be in town three days a week for classes."

"I..." Iris looked down at the papers again, then back at James. Something shifted in her expression as understanding dawned. "This isn't just about the course, is it?"

"No," he admitted. "It's not."

He was vaguely aware of Mrs. Lucy quietly ushering everyone else into the parlor, giving them a moment of privacy in the kitchen. But his entire world had narrowed to Iris's face, to the way she was looking at him as if she could see right through to his soul.

"Iris Green," he began, his voice rough with emotion, "I came to this farm looking for work, but I found so much more. I found a home. A family. And most importantly, I found you."

Her hands trembled in his as he continued.

"You are the most remarkable woman I've ever known. You're brilliant and stubborn and kind, and you deserve every dream you've ever had to put aside. I want to give you those dreams. I want to build a life with you where you can be everything you are meant to be."

He released one of her hands to reach for the ring box, sinking to one knee on the kitchen floor.

"I love you," he said simply. "I love your determination and your strength. I love how you check on the pigs every night even when you don't have to. I love watching you teach Anna Latin and mathematics. I love that you're never afraid to tell me when I'm wrong."

"I love that you took a chance on a wandering farmhand who dared to rearrange your pig pens. And I'm asking you to take another chance now." He opened the box, revealing his mother's ring. "Marry me?"

Iris stared at the ring, then at him, tears spilling freely now. "You ridiculous man," she whispered. "Did you really think I'd say anything but yes?"

"Is that a yes then?" His heart felt like it might burst.

"Yes," she laughed through her tears. "Yes, I'll marry you, James Brown, you impossibly wonderful man."

He slipped the ring onto her finger with shaking hands, then stood and pulled her close, not caring who might see through the kitchen window.

"I love you," she whispered against his lips.

A cheer erupted from the parlor doorway where

their family had gathered to watch. Anna rushed forward first, throwing her arms around them both.

"Finally!" she exclaimed. "I've been keeping this secret for weeks!"

"Weeks?" Iris pulled back to look at her sister. "How many people knew about this?"

"Oh, everyone," Anna said cheerfully. "Even the pigs probably knew. James is terrible at being subtle."

"I am not," James protested, but everyone's laughter suggested otherwise.

Mrs. Lucy wiped tears from her eyes as she approached. "I think this calls for something stronger than tea," she announced, producing a bottle of champagne from her basket.

"Mrs. Lucy!" Iris gasped in mock scandal. "Have you been hiding champagne in your library basket?"

"My dear girl," Mrs. Lucy's eyes twinkled, "where do you think I've been hiding all those 'forbidden' novels all these years?"

As Henry poured the champagne and Mrs. Lucy produced a cake that definitely hadn't been made by Anna, James kept his arm around Iris's waist, unwilling to let go just yet.

"Happy?" he murmured against her hair.

She turned in his embrace, her eyes bright with

joy and possibility. "Deliriously," she assured him. "Though I do have one condition."

"Anything."

"When I finish my course and start working..."

"Yes?"

"You have to promise to let me handle all the farm's legal documents." Her smile turned mischievous. "Your handwriting is atrocious."

James laughed, pulling her closer. "I wouldn't have it any other way."

CHAPTER 17

EPILOGUE

Six years had passed since he'd first walked these paths as a hired hand, yet every morning still felt like a gift. The farm had flourished beyond their wildest dreams, with the Yorkshire breeding program now renowned throughout the county.

James paused by Henry's favorite oak tree, its branches spreading wide over the newly expanded pig pens. The old man had loved sitting here in his final years, watching his grandchild toddle after the piglets while sharing stories of Annie with anyone who'd listen. The memory squeezed James's heart - it had been seven months since they'd laid Henry to rest beside his beloved wife, but the ache still felt fresh.

"Papa!" A small voice called out. "The big pig is doing it again!"

James turned to see his four-year-old son, Henry James Brown (though everyone called him Harry), pointing excitedly at their prize Yorkshire boar. The boy's copper curls caught the sunlight, so like his mother's it made James's chest tight.

"Doing what, exactly?" James made his way to where Harry bounced on his toes by the fence.

"Making his happy noise!" Harry demonstrated with a surprisingly accurate imitation of a pig's contented grunt. "Just like you taught me!"

"That's because he knows it's feeding time." James scooped up his son, settling him on his hip. "Want to help?"

"Can I really?" Harry's green eyes - another inheritance from Iris - widened with delight.

"Of course. Though we should probably check with your mother first. Where is she?"

"Mama's doing her important papers in Grandfather's study." Harry's face turned serious. "Aunt Anna says we mustn't disturb her when she's doing sums."

James smiled, remembering how Iris had transformed Henry's old study into her own workspace. She split her time now between the farm accounts and her position at Howard & Sons Accountancy in town.

"Well then," James adjusted Harry on his hip, "what do you say we surprise her with breakfast when she's finished? I hear Aunt Anna might have baked fresh bread before leaving for her teaching post."

"With blackberry jam?" Harry asked hopefully.

"Is there any other kind worth eating?"

They made their way to the feed storage, Harry "helped" measure portions with all the solemn concentration a four-year-old could muster. James watched his son carefully count scoops (missing several numbers but making up for it with enthusiasm), marveling at how naturally he took to farm life.

"Papa?" Harry asked as they distributed feed among the pens. "Why did Grandfather like this tree so much?"

James paused, looking up at the oak's sprawling branches. "Well, your grandfather first met your grandmother under this tree. She was reading under the tree when her father's pigs got loose. Your grandfather helped catch them, and the rest..." He smiled at the memory of Henry telling this story. "The rest is our family's history."

"Is that why Mama comes here sometimes? To remember?"

"Yes, love." James's throat tightened. "And to feel close to them both."

"I miss him," Harry said simply, patting the tree trunk with a small hand. "He told the best stories."

"That he did." James ruffled his son's curls. "And now I and your mama will tell those stories to you."

They finished the feeding rounds just as the sun cleared. James could see movement in the study window now. Iris would be coming out soon, ready to head into town for her afternoon at the accountancy.

"Race you to the kitchen?" he suggested to Harry.

"But Mama says no running near the pigs!"

"Ah, but we're not near the pigs anymore, are we?"

Harry's face lit up with delighted conspiracy. "Last one there has to clean the pig pens!"

"Oh" James let his son get a head start, Harry's laughter trailing behind him as they raced across the yard.

The kitchen was warm and fragrant with the smell of Anna's baking when they burst in. True to form, a fresh loaf sat cooling on the rack, along with a note in Anna's elegant teacher's hand: "For my favorite nephew (and his tolerably decent parents). Don't let Harry eat it all at once."

"Too late!" Harry reached for the bread, but James caught him around the waist.

"Hands washed first, young man. What would your Aunt Anna say?"

"She'd say that cleanliness is next to godliness," Iris's voice came from the doorway, "and that little boys who want to be pig farmers must be especially clean."

James's heart did that familiar skip at the sight of her. Five years of marriage hadn't dimmed the effect she had on him. She wore one of her "town dresses" now, proper and professional, but her hair still escaped its pins in copper wisps that begged to be tucked back.

"Mama!" Harry squirmed free of James's grasp and ran to her. "Papa let me help with the feeding! I counted all the scoops and everything!"

"Did he now?" Iris caught their son up in her arms, raising an eyebrow at James. "And did Papa remember that someone has lessons with Mrs. Lucy this morning?"

"Lessons?" Harry's face fell. "But I want to help with the pigs!"

"Even pig farmers need to read," Iris reminded him gently. "Your grandfather taught me that. He'd be so proud to see you learning your letters."

Harry considered this seriously. "Did Grandfather like books?"

"He loved them." Iris carried him to the wash basin, helping him clean his hands. "Especially after your Papa taught him new farming methods. He read everything he could find about it."

"It's true," James added, starting to slice the bread. "He used to say that a good farmer needs both practical experience and book learning. That's why your Mama went to secretarial school, and why Aunt Anna became a teacher."

"And why you have to wash behind your ears," Iris tickled Harry's neck, making him giggle. "Mrs. Lucy won't want a grubby student."

As they settled around the kitchen table - the same one where James had first shared meals with the Greens - he watched Iris butter a slice of bread for their son. She moved with such natural grace between her roles: mother, accountant, farmer's wife. She'd taken on each new challenge with the same determination she'd shown that first day he'd met her.

"I reviewed the quarterly accounts this morning," she said, accepting the cup of tea James passed her. "The new breeding pair is already showing excellent returns."

"I told you they would." He couldn't resist. "Almost like someone with experience in pig farming might know what he's talking about."

"Don't get smug, Mr. Brown." But her eyes sparkled. "I seem to recall someone insisting that the south field wouldn't support turnips."

"One mistake in five years and she never lets me forget it."

"Never," she agreed cheerfully. "Though I suppose you've made up for it in other ways."

Their eyes met across the table, years of shared joy and grief and triumph passing between them. Harry, oblivious to the moment, happily smeared jam across his bread with more enthusiasm than precision.

"I have news from town," Iris said after a moment. "Mr. Howard is retiring."

James set down his cup. "The Howard of Howard & Sons?"

She nodded. "He offered me partnership in the

firm. It would mean more responsibility, but also more flexibility with my hours." She glanced at Harry, then back to James. "I'd be home more, able to help more with the farm while still maintaining my own career."

"Iris, that's wonderful!" James reached across the table to squeeze her hand. "Your father would have been so proud."

"I know." She blinked rapidly. "I keep wanting to tell him. To see his face when..." She trailed off, composing herself.

"He knew," James said softly. "He watched you build all this, the farm, your career, our family. He knew exactly how remarkable you are."

"Papa?" Harry interrupted, face serious. "Why is Mama crying?"

"Because sometimes," James explained, "when we miss people we love very much, our hearts get so full that it spills out through our eyes."

Harry nodded sagely. "Like when Aunt Anna cried at harvest fair because the pig won a ribbon and Grandfather wasn't there to see?"

"Exactly like that." Iris wiped her eyes, smiling at their son.

James watched her with a tenderness that never seemed to fade, even after all these years. His heart swelled with love for this woman who had been his steadfast companion through every season of life. She was not only his wife but the very heart of everything they had built.

James took Iris's hand, his heart full. "I love you," he said softly.

She smiled, her eyes meeting his. "I love you, too."

ALSO BY SYBIL COOK

The Farrier's Daughter

In a world defined by duty and hardship, can love be the escape that leads to a future worth fighting for?

In the heart of the English countryside, Enid Boothe's life is shaped by duty and hardship. As the daughter of a farrier, she helps care for her many siblings while managing the demands of a humble home. With sickness and financial struggle weighing heavily on the family, Enid's world begins to shift when she meets Jack Greenwood, a young groundsman at the nearby Braley House. Despite her deep sense of responsibility and the turmoil at home, Enid is drawn to Jack's kindness and the lightness he brings to her otherwise grim life.

As their bond grows, so does the pressure on Enid's family. When her father loses his job and her mother's health declines, Enid is forced to confront the impossible choice between caring for her family and pursuing the future she dreams of with Jack. Just as things seem hopeless, a chance opportunity at the Big House offers Enid a new path forward, but it comes at the cost of her dreams of escape.

As Enid learns new skills and supports her family, her

love for Jack continues to grow. With her father finding new work and the weight of their struggles finally easing, Enid and Jack's love story blooms into a future neither of them ever thought possible. But will Enid's loyalty to her family and her desire for a better life collide, or will love and perseverance lead them to a brighter future?

DOWNLOAD NOW

Printed in Great Britain
by Amazon